PRAISE FOR
The Year of the Return

"Nathaniel Popkin unveils a vivid tapestry woven from the conjoined histories of two American families. United by marriage, the Jewish Silks and the African-American Johnsons struggle to navigate their blended worlds in the wake of a devastating loss. Thankfully, Popkin avoids the usual pitfalls that gobble up so many authors who try to write about "race," focusing instead on what is universal and relatable about his characters' emotions rather than easy stereotypes. Set during the run-up to Philadelphia's Bicentennial celebrations, *The Year of the Return* grabbed me from the first page and I dove deep, careening between enchantment and the terrors experienced by multiple characters as they tackle questions of identity, racial culpability, and even the true cost of war. In keeping with the Bicentennial setting, the story even inspires a surge of patriotism: Not the repugnant Nationalism so prevalent these days, but the hard-won patriotism of the immigrant, the *outsider*; the patriotism of the enslaved peoples who worked for free and died for their children's share of the American Dream. Popkin tells a deeply satisfying story of damaged heroes grasping toward the promise of a better tomorrow. He also delves unerringly into the dark nature of human ambition, racism and, ultimately, the transcendent power of hope. In an era where cynicism is easy, the better angels at play within these pages filled me with yearning, not for an America that never was, but for the America that might still be possible."

—Michael Boatman,
Screen actor and author of *Who Wants to Be The Prince of Darkness?*

"A beautiful, absorbing novel about the crisis of American cities in the twentieth century, *The Year of the Return* is remarkable for its generous and intimate approach to politics. A complex portrait of a family at a pivotal moment, it also sensitively and knowledgeably presents the historical failures that led to our current political chaos."

—Sandra Newman, author of *The Heavens*

"Emotionally honest, authentically rendered. *The Year of the Return* deftly shifts narratives to tell the intertwined stories of the Johnsons and the Silks, the interracial marriage that inextricably binds them, the loss that shatters them. Nathaniel Popkin has crafted a novel that is both haunting and graceful with a soulfulness that lingers."

—Diane McKinney-Whetstone, author of *Lazaretto*

"With the compassion of a storyteller and the exacting eye of an historian, Nathaniel Popkin brings to life Philadelphia in the 1970s in this immersive, propulsive read. Entertaining, edifying, and relevant."

—Elise Juska, author of *If We Had Known*

"A complex, polyphonic dive into personal and societal grief. Popkin expertly shepherds us through a recent yet forgotten time in Philadelphia, whose lessons are particularly resonant today."

—Vikram Paralkar, author of *Night Theater*

The Year of the Return

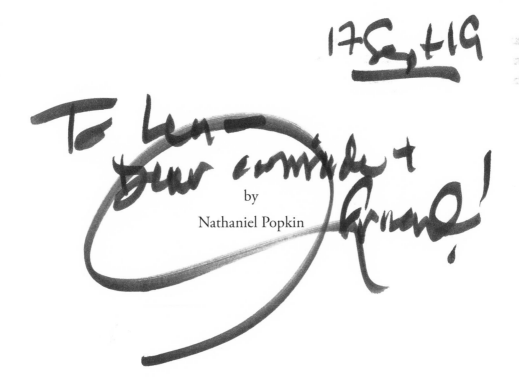

by

Nathaniel Popkin

Also by the Author

Fiction

Everything is Borrowed
Lion and Leopard

Non-Fiction

Finding the Hidden City (with Joseph E.B. Elliott and Peter Woodall)
The Possible City
Song of the City

Anthology
Who Will Speak for America? (edited with Stephanie Feldman)

Published by Open Books

Copyright © 2019 by Nathaniel Popkin

Interior design by Siva Ram Maganti

Cover images © koyash07 White shutterstock.com/g/koyash

ISBN-13: 978-1948598194

To my sister Nancy

"He sat there alone in the darkness of his soul
and decided to rewrite his story."

Elias Khoury, *Broken Mirrors: Sinalcol*

Silk Family

Sam Silk, *owner of Silk Industries, husband of Harriett, father of Alan and Paul*

Harriett Birnbaum Silk, *English teacher, wife of Sam, mother of Alan and Paul*

Alan Silk, *insurance executive, eldest child of Sam and Harriett*

Paul Silk, *newspaper editor, second child of Sam and Harriett, widowed husband of Charlene Johnson*

Albert Birnbaum, *attorney, brother of Harriett*

Simone Feld Birnbaum, *photographer, mother of Harriett and Albert, maternal grandmother of Alan and Paul*

Betty Gordon Silk, *mother of Sam Silk, paternal grandmother of Alan and Paul*

Harry Silk, *brother of Betty's deceased husband Abe, uncle of Sam*

Johnson Family

Charles Johnson, *Tasty Baking delivery truck driver, husband of Anita, father of Charlene, Monte, and Jeanette*

Anita Smith Johnson, *employee of the Social Security Administration, wife of Charles, mother of Charlene, Monte, and Jeanette*

Charlene Johnson Silk, *eldest child of Charles and Anita, late wife of Paul Silk*

Monte Johnson, *Vietnam War veteran, second child of Charles and Anita*

Jeanette Johnson, *dental office receptionist, third child of Charles and Anita*

Elsa Franklin Smith, *retired shopkeeper, mother of Anita, maternal grandmother of Charlene, Monte, and Jeanette*

Other Characters

Michael Olivetti, *second-generation owner of pizza restaurant*
Louis Turner, *employee of Silk Industries*
Eddie Williams, *employee of Silk Industries*
Susan Painter, *actor, director, dancer*

Prologue:
The Lebanon Arms

Harry Silk

You're asking me where I live? I live on the planet Xylon in the eighth dimension and I eat powdered sugar all day out of a giant wooden scoop made by a French baker, a friend of Voltaire. An old Kraut lady, Frau Heckel (like freckle) comes in and cleans. She wears her hair in pigtails. So she isn't old at all. Except she has the same sound to her voice as every complicit Nazi housewife. This is my nightmare, do you understand? Don't look so ashen, kid.

I check in on my sister-in-law Betty every day, like clockwork. This isn't so heroic. We both live on the eighth floor of the Lebanon Arms. She's in 803 and I'm in 812. Opposite sides of the floor. We live in the tallest building in Wynnefield. They should have named Philadelphia New Wales, or New West Wales. (You follow?) Now I see some color returning to your face.

I'm just an old hardware man unlike my brother Abe, Mr. Silk. Mr. Silk of Silk Industries. When Abe went to heaven in 1966 (that is a joke, Jews don't believe in heaven or hell) the Lebanon Arms was brand-new and Betty, always a woman of distinction (I say so sincerely), so different from my Fanny, who was, God bless her, always content to be in the store, behind the counter next to me—So Betty moved in. Naturally she chose an apartment with two balconies with lavish views of the park and the city. Abe had left her enough to hire a decorator and, anyway, her son, Sam, the new chief of Silk Industries, continued to pay her a small salary. Now God has seen to it that the heiress and the hardware man live on the same floor.

I go over around one-thirty, after my sister-in-law has had her tuna salad and cottage cheese. My visit will arouse her sufficiently that she'll make me coffee. The girl is tall and overweight, with a head like a parking cone. Every day, when she opens the door to the apartment (I always ring instead of using my key—no one should accuse me of breaking in), I get a picture in my head of a giant zucchini. But once I settle into the kitchen and start wiping the crumbs off the tablecloth, she takes her lunch break and leaves.

About the time the coffee has cooled sufficiently Betty will stop making sense (I see the look in your eyes) or she may doze off. I'll do the crossword puzzle in the paper and when she lifts her eyelids and notices me she'll think to complain about Harriett rifling through the papers on her desk. I'll counsel her to arrange the papers in a certain way and advise her to leave them out—lay a trap. I may even prod her, in which case she'll respond in a stern voice. "Why is she going through your papers," I'll say, innocently. "Because she wants to get her hands on my money." When she says this she no longer sounds like Betty, a kind and graceful woman (my brother Abe chose well). Actually she sounds a bit like Harriett.

The truth is it's me who goes through her papers, the hardware man God has chosen to take up residence on the eighth floor of the Lebanon Arms, to live among the stars.

Betty Silk

My grandson Paul came to visit me today. He came right up in the elevator without even calling up and I had the girl let him in. I couldn't understand it because on a Monday he should be in school, but the girl said, in that stern voice I can't stand, that he was a grown man and that he'd just moved back to town. I'm not sure how she knew all this but the important thing was that I get dressed properly and fix my hair and the girl dabbed on a little blush.

He is a handsome boy, his hair thick and wavy like my late husband's was, may you rest in peace, Abe, my angel, and he has the same eyes, like deep green pools. I think Sam's eyes are just the same. "Sit," I said, "sit and let me get you a cup of coffee," which I did myself since she doesn't know how to do it right, it always tastes a little bitter when she makes it, and I wanted my boy to have a good cup of coffee to remember me by, and some orange Milanos, which are his favorite. My boy said he'd just arrived the night before and I couldn't understand this. From vacation? And where is Harriett? Paul, this is Paul, someone said. My grandson Paul. A grown man! A handsome man. "How nice of you to visit, you know everyone forgets me up here, I have to call and call to get your wife to visit."

He leaned in to me then, the kind boy, so close I could almost feel his whiskers on my cheek. When Harriett comes in here she doesn't even sit, she's probably going through my papers. I told my son about it, she goes right for my desk drawers. Well this boy leaned in and he took my hands, and he seemed to wipe a tear from his eye, and he said, "Nana, it's me, Paul. I've moved back home from Denver and that's because my wife, Charlene, you remember Charlene? Charlene, my wife, died. She had cancer."

I couldn't believe this. That's what I told him. I can't believe it.

1.

Seeking Monte

Elsa Franklin Smith

Years ago, before I moved in here with my daughter and son-in-law, Charles would come home from his route just after three to be home for those kids. Charles was proud of that job, because he got it even before the boycott that Reverend Sullivan led to force the owners of Tasty Baking to hire more Negro men. Charles was proud because he got the job on his own merit and because his getting the job "kicked open the door," he liked to say, to the others. Men of his generation are always in need of a little recognition. I always said Charles deserved it. And he did. And he came home when the route was done, after dropping the truck back on Hunting Park Avenue, as they did in those days—they weren't allowed to bring them home. And then he had to catch three buses before they bought the Ford and he drove himself. He got home before the kids did and he made sure they had something to eat and did their homework.

Now he brings the truck home and he's to keep track of the gas and the mileage. But I think he drives it around a while now, or he pulls it up on Lancaster Avenue and he sits himself at a bar afraid to come home. He's afraid to see what Monte's gotten into. But I'm here and I can see. Charles will come home and ask, "Where's Monte?" or did Monte do this or that. He's over on such-and-such corner, I'll have to say.

When Charles comes home today, and when Anita comes in from

1

the Social Security office where she works, will I tell them what I've heard? Around one o'clock I received a telephone call. I was making chicken salad when the phone rang. It was a familiar voice that made me light-headed when I realized who it was and I pulled the chair over and sat there with the phone and the cord stretched tight. Paul was on the line. He called to speak to me? He must have known only I would be at home then. Me or Monte. But Paul couldn't have known whether Monte was working or not. Such long silences when he's talking, long and quiet pauses, like a cloud passing across the sun, and during those pauses I told him how everyone was. I asked if he was calling from Denver. I nearly choked up on that word, that city. He heard this, I am near certain, and Paul being Paul his voice grew quieter, like a dimming flame, but a flame still hot, and he wondered if I would have a sandwich or a coffee with him. He isn't in Denver anymore, he said. He repeated that word, Denver, on purpose for some reason, possibly to show he wasn't trying to run away from it, or because for Paul Denver means Charlene, as if they were the same two words. Because he'd left Denver but not Charlene and he was living home now, at his parents' new house. "All the way in Bala," he said. I laughed and said, "Paul, it's only a mile-and-a-half away." And he said, "Yes, Granny, but it feels like another world." "It's a beautiful new house and your mother has such wonderful taste." We made a date for next Wednesday. Before we got off he asked, again, if I was sure it was all right. He isn't false that boy. I mean he doesn't fake it, as some people do. It's easy to understand how Charlene could never say no.

Charles Johnson

Sometimes when I'm finished my route, I come back up from the lower end of Lancaster Avenue and then pull over at the mess of weed trees near 55th, all that junk by the tracks, and kill the engine. I turn on my transistor radio, close my eyes, and I'll take whatever's shaking out of Philly International that WDAS will air. It doesn't matter if it's Patti LaBelle or Lou Rawls or Harold Melvin and the

Blue Notes, whichever one is hot they play over and over. I close my eyes and all those people I lost come back to me. I can feel them on my skin and I'm no spiritual kind of cat. The Tasty Kake truck has a fake sweet smell and even that might dissolve if it's just a little warm and I can open the window. The thing about this spot is that it catches the sun at that late time of day. I lost quite a few of them in the Pacific, more in the Pacific than the Atlantic. I was one of the few to see action in both. At first you can't live without those people. But after some time, even the ones who survive—you lose them, too.

This is where they collect, though—man, I can't let them in anywhere else. Charlene, she comes here and sits with me, like we used to go down and sit on Belmont Plateau when she was five, 1952. Me and her: we made up songs about the kings and queens who lived in the house with the fairy tale name, Strawberry Mansion. I knew the house had been a stop on the Underground Railroad, but still we sang about kings and queens.

Her mama comes in—she's allowed, too. She wasn't always, but now I do myself a favor and admit she's lost, lost in her own sweet world. It isn't sweet, more like acid since the funeral, like some clear chemical you think won't hurt you. She comes to me here and I apologize. She lets me tell her I'm sorry. Inside the delivery truck is the only place left where that can happen. I'm sorry that girl of ours is gone. I'm sorry what that's done to me. The old Charles would keep you near, could draw you back along the line. This one makes his deliveries. And if he's got anything left it goes to Monte.

The kid's asleep when I get up, if he's even here, gone when I come home, I know he's avoiding me—mother and son are good at that. He's just as peculiar as she is. Gotten worse, bent in on himself. He was born in 1951 and I could have named him Jackie, or even, by then, July, Willie. But I knew he had to be Monte. I'd seen that cat, Monte Irvin, in the Negro Leagues playing for Jersey City. 1950 was his first full year in the bigs. Hit .299, knocked in sixty-six for the Giants. I'm watching him in the paper every day and even on my block some of them are saying, You know these crackers ain't so bad. The so-called Whiz Kids. White Kids, as bleached out as this truck. Then fifty-one comes and I'm already looking to see what Monte Irvin's up to. He's good and he's got Willie, now, too, and together they're all right. Only thing is they'll never catch Jackie and the Dodgers. But I had faith when I named my boy Monte.

Now, sometimes I'll spot him from here inside my truck, down in this part of the neighborhood. Crossing the street like a death spider. I'm not exactly sure what he's messing with. Everybody knows the smell test. That weed does stink. Better than the fake sweet smell of this truck. That's a real sweet smell, but I'm saying, I don't smell it. Not on him. Not on that kid. So what? That mean he's doing something else? Lot of 'em touching the dope, the real dope. I asked him, What'd you get into over there? The U.S. Government sends these kids over there, teaches 'em to kill, gets up in their heads, and then gets 'em hooked? Hooked hard. You got tracks on your arms, son? I look in on him in the morning. I go in there. I don't care. He's dead to the world. I don't see any tracks. So then, what? You selling? I ask Granny, she watches him too. Like a hawk that woman. Got eyes all over her head. But she won't say a thing—that family holds everything inside. If he's selling then I need to sit up, turn the engine on, and plant myself there outside his spot? Use this truck like a big old body, get in the way. I have to find it first, find it before Rizzo does. No Rizzo cop better be coming for my son, not now. Not this time. He done his time. He paid with his mind. Stay away from my kid!

Lord, I'm no praying man. This is my church, this foul-smelling truck. Damn. The smell of white heaven.

Monte was born July 5, 1951. On that day Monte Irvin's Giants were seven games behind the Dodgers. August 11, they were back thirteen. Everybody knows what happened then. Monte hit .312. Ended the season with twenty-four homers and 121 RBIs. The Giants won the pennant. Nobody before or since has come back from so far behind.

Elsa Franklin Smith

My full name is Elsa Franklin Smith and I've lived here in this city since I was six. That was seventy years ago, in 1906. My father heard about a place, a giant factory that made children's toys, little pianos, puppets, ice skates, and sleds. Though I'm quite sure he'd never had such a toy in his life. He heard he could get a job making them. That's the kind of man my father was. He dreamed of making children's toys.

My mother wasn't a dreamer and as soon as they arrived here from Petersburg, Virginia and she realized she had to feed me and find me a school to attend, she took a job with a family on Pine Street, a very proper home with proper rooms and a piano, a concert piano, and a library with wood paneling like they used to have. She took the position with Dr. Wilson, a very prominent doctor and a professor, too. My mother had gone to school in Virginia until the sixth grade and so she could read pretty well and the Doctor's wife appreciated this, I gather. But mostly my mother did the domestic chores. She did the cleaning and the wash and the marketing while I went to school. I went to the Ohio Street School for the first two years, which wasn't on Ohio Street at all but on Lombard Street and right next to Lombard was Pine. But even so I wasn't allowed to bother my mother when she was working, only once in a while on a holiday I was allowed to go with her and help, of course. But my father's mother came north after a short time and she stayed with us and watched after me. And I called her Granny just like these kids have always called me. She didn't say much, just hummed the spirituals and kept an eye out to make sure I was safe.

Then she passed one day. This was soon after I had started at the Durham School, the great big new school with giant windows for Negro children. That's when I saw my father cry and I came to see despair the first time. He was always so happy and optimistic, much like Charles. And like Charles, the darkness could overcome him.

Charles has his opinions. My son-in-law prides himself I gather on being the discerning type of man. He comes from old stock. When I was a girl they called them Old Philadelphians. I thought that meant they were like Grampa Sherman, shriveled up like a raisin. I thought all old people shriveled like a raisin meant you were born a slave. But somehow Old Philadelphian meant the opposite, you come from freedom. Johnsons were half-Haitian and they were cooks and porters. They never came from behind. Maybe my father couldn't be that way. He never got that job in the toy factory. I imagine the factory didn't exist, or if it did they didn't give out jobs to Negro men. So he had to find another way.

Now Charles has me worried. He used to be awfully patriotic, and the Bicentennial is coming. The old Charles would be as excited as I am for our nation's birthday right here in our city, the birthplace of America, and even more given his service. He isn't cynical about it and neither am I. I told him, no one can take it away from us, not Nixon, this was before he had to resign, not even Frank Rizzo. I'm going with bells on, I don't care how hot it is on the Fourth of July. The heat hasn't ever bothered me. I haven't lived this long only to decide it doesn't matter. My father did get a job, and he held it for years, in the pressroom of the Record. That job wasn't any old job because he knew it had a purpose. If ever I came to see him there he would excuse himself and take me around the corner to Independence Hall. We would stand there under the arcade, and he would say, "Elsa, as long as you live remember this is yours." Lately seems like Charles has been made to forget who he is. And I've seen Anita withdraw. When I see her that way and not able to give him comfort, smile or the touch of the hand, I feel it's my responsibility. Oh, I don't know if things are all right with him or not, or what kind of wife she's ever been, and I can tell all this has weighed down on her just as much as him, only differently. First my beautiful and intelligent Charlene and now Monte. Three years he's been back from Vietnam and still he's lost, afraid of himself, I gather. And sometimes I think we should be afraid of him, no matter how gentle he always was, how fine. I worry over that boy and look at his mother and she can't figure out what to do so she just looks at him. What can you say to a boy who's been to war, and not just a war, a war without any sense to it? That boy didn't want to hurt anyone. He had some peculiar ideas, but all young men have their ideas, their notions, and that's their right. I can't tell a boy who's been off to war what to do. And no one can stop him from doing whatever he's going to do. It's a shame, a terrible shame, to let the boy get caught up in the street.

I've always been the observing type, our customers would say, Miss Elsa's always watching. At first I thought it must be drugs. He had that afro when he first came home, twice the size it is today. It was like clown hair only he was no clown. He couldn't be a clown. Was he doing drugs or selling them? Was he stealing? Now I don't know if he isn't part of that Black Mafia. I make him sit in front of me and I look him over, and I see what's going on, but I can only tell so much. Whatever it is, I don't like it.

Monte Johnson

If you want to know a few things:

1. I weigh the same now as I did the day I was drafted, on my eighteenth birthday, July 5, 1969.

2. Growing up in Philadelphia didn't prepare me for the humidity of the jungle or what it feels like to breathe fire in your lungs.

3. Number two (2) is partially a joke.

4. Under certain circumstances (war), a man's intestines can unravel.

5. I burned all the drawings I made.

6. Number five (5) contains an inaccuracy. A redneck from Arkansas in my division burned my drawings. That was in 1970. He later became my best friend. My best friend has one arm (now).

7. The first time I smoked grass was in the tenth grade at a debate tournament at Central High School. On the south lawn.

8. Frank Rizzo.

9. My sister Jeanette has never smoked grass.

10. I was a cherry boy. All I could think of was other cherries and so I tried to stay clean. Clean in mind and clean in body!

11. I missed Charlene's wedding (war) and I almost missed her funeral.

12. My daddy is no saint.

13. (Lucky 13) My brother-in-law (is he still my brother-in-law?) Paul is here in Philadelphia right now. I spotted him and Granny getting off the trolley and crossing 63rd Street. I couldn't see from my vantage point, but I think he brought her right up to our door.

Charles Johnson

Spring training only got going last week and already they've got Phillies plastered all over our trucks, that new mascot, the guy who looks like a frog, a white frog not a green one, supposed to be William Penn or something. And a girl with yellow hair and a baseball glove on her hand. Both these cats dressed like 1776. As if I'm supposed to care about the Bicentennial. Two-hundred years and my kid's still the one being sacrificed? And I'm driving my route, pretty much everything north of Lancaster Avenue, and everything along Lancaster, too, where some of my best customers are, with this on my truck, like I want to be doing the Phillies' business for them. They ain't paying me! They got poor old Dick Allen for that and that old cat strikes out once every night, but he's their man. And he comes back for more. Must have his reasons. This centerfielder with the long legs is something. I'll give 'em that. Willie Mays taught him what's up and showed him how to cover ground. I won't watch the Phillies, but I will watch the centerfielder. I keep my eye on him. I told Monte about the centerfielder, but talking to him is like talking to a wall. He looks at me like I'm the one who made the world like it is and never did anything about it; shit, I can't even bring the truck home and park it on the block because I'll just catch hell from him. Well, the old Monte would give me hell for the Phillies junk all over the truck and this Monte here barely seems to notice, he's so shut up inside himself. If I could do one thing with my life again it would be to break that kid's leg so he wouldn't go to Nam.

Only my son goes to the jungle to stay out of trouble. Nah, that ain't true either. This neighborhood is filled with kids trying to escape. But Monte didn't go and serve to be like his daddy. He went because he was stalked, lined up, stripped, and treated like an animal by Mr. Frank Rizzo. For pointing out the truth.

The shame of it is I never worried about these kids. I always told Anita, "They're all right, they're gonna be all right. They got good heads." I mean, Jeanette tells me everyday nothing's going to stop her. Charlene always knew what she wanted and how to steer clear of trouble. Even when she tells us she's going to marry Paul and they're going to move west, to Denver. Denver? But she says, "It's 1969, Daddy, and we can't live here." I never gave it a second thought. He proved himself all right and I'm not in the business of saying no.

Paul Silk

"I understand why Charlene could never say no to you, Paul," Granny said, and took my hands in hers.

"But she said no to me all the time," I replied. "It was her idea to leave, you know." I stopped, looked up, and started again. "She said we can't live here, this city—'this city has race fever,' and they would never let us live in peace. She was right. Denver seemed to her that it must be transparent, the thin mountain air maybe. Well, it turns out they have a different history."

Of course you were right, Charlene. Now I'm back here and you're everywhere, just the same, in the brick and in the steam. In the tilt of Granny's head, across from me in the dim blood light.

But Granny didn't believe me. She grimaced. She didn't believe it was your idea. You know Granny loves Peking duck and we were sitting in a dark booth in a stifling place on Race Street. The booths and Formica tables and walls were all red. The lampshades were red. The ducks hung in the window. They were red. "Do you think I'm that persuasive?" I said and Granny grimaced again. Then for just a moment I forgot you had gone: this was the strange power of the color red.

"The cops, Rizzo's cops," I managed to say. "And now he's Mayor.

She never wanted you to know." Will you forgive me, Charlene?

"Don't worry about Granny's ears."

"She was a cub reporter, really an intern. That was her title. But they knew she was on the team investigating police brutality. They went after her because she was young, and a woman, and black. She stood up to them."

"You mean they threatened her?"

You stood up to them even when they called you a whore, Charlene, and me your pimp, and pushed me up against the statue of General McClellan. And the weasel backup groped you. You stayed quiet and calm and it was me who said, "You're just proving yourselves," which they didn't even understand.

"Outside City Hall one night, a cold March night when it should have been spring. We held close to each other to keep warm."

It was freezing and they took their time looking over our drivers' licenses, as if they needed to know who we were. They knew exactly. But you stayed calm and quiet and you needed me to do the same, but I couldn't.

"I lost my composure when they tried to intimidate us."

"It was your passion she loved," Granny said. "She needed that fire. She wouldn't ever say it, but we knew. But, Paul, you didn't get in some kind of trouble for it that night, did you?"

They weren't going to get away with it. I told them I had their badge numbers and I was going directly to the 52nd Ward Committee, to the Ward Leader, a friend of my father, and the newspaper wouldn't be silent. But you knew this was a mistake—it could derail the entire investigation. They laughed in my face. We weren't anywhere near the 52nd Ward. It was a hollow threat, but still, you soothed me. You soothed me, Charlene, and then you whispered in my ear, "We were going to have to leave, baby."

"Charlene kept the cool. The cops—they never seemed to realize this would become part of the newspaper's investigation, too. But really she couldn't bear it and I couldn't see it. I was as blind and stupid as the cops."

Granny tried to tell me it wasn't so, but I didn't want to talk about

myself. I asked about her health (the usual arthritis, an old heart mur-
mur I'd never heard about), your mama and daddy, Jeanette, Monte.
Your mama's become even more withdrawn, and your daddy a little
lost (she's seen him sitting in the driver's seat of his truck staring into
nothing), and Jeanette? "You never quite know with that girl. She never
stops moving—" Granny never finished the sentence. She took a sip
of the iced tea that came in a red glass with a red straw. For a moment
she appeared old, in the sense of geological time, an ancient being.

"You're afraid to tell me about Monte," I said.

"I don't know how you use those chopsticks."

"When you live with a vegetarian you eat a lot of Chinese food,"
I answered, forgetting, again, and in the forgetting losing track of
Monte. As soon as I said "vegetarian" my throat constricted. I tried
to hold back. I'm accustomed to the pain and yet, still, it surprises.
Will it always surprise? I leaned in closer to Granny, determined.
"Monte's gotten into drugs? Stealing? Pimping?" The words seemed
to come from somewhere. Granny didn't indicate one way or the
other. She chewed, she stopped chewing.

"They aren't the same when they come home."

"Not anyone is like Monte." Granny shook her head.

"He admired his sister most of all," she said.

"She knew that," I responded too quickly. I wasn't lying but I felt
like I was covering something over, Charlene, filling a hole I hadn't
made. A hole I'd been ordered to fill. I could trace the hole to 1969,
the year we decided to leave. Monte's draft number came up in the
summer. No, the hole must have started before. He went off in early
1970. He didn't call to say goodbye. You called him, we both talked
to him, but he was distant. His voice was already far away. Maybe
you weren't prepared for the worry. At the *Post* you interviewed returning vets. "They're all afraid to talk," you said, but Monte was
afraid before he left. And you didn't press him. Then he went missing
and he didn't arrive home at 63rd and Lebanon until almost the end
of 1972. That's when we came home for Christmas. But when we
arrived at your house Monte wouldn't come down. He was locked in
his old room. Do you remember, we almost tried to break the lock?

Why were we so desperate, Charlene? He'd been to war—everything was fraught. Your mama was crying downstairs. So we retreated and you put your arms around her and your daddy handed me a beer. Jeanette walked in and we rushed to see her. It had been two years, at least. She'd graduated Overbrook and was working in a shoe shop on Chestnut Street. For a minute we must have forgotten about Monte and that's when he appeared, Charlene, in one of your old dresses and his great, giant afro, and tattoos on his arms.

"Please stop!" you shouted. And then, more sternly, "Don't do this." You couldn't see him as any kind of victim, if that's in fact what he was. The whole week of Christmas we never saw him again.

"He hasn't gotten over any of it," Granny remarked. It was war. It was more than war.

"Granny, I'm going to find him."

Granny took my arm as we walked toward Market Street. I found it hard to discern her voice in the din of traffic, jackhammering, the groan of the diesel buses. Someone was banging a drum. Granny didn't seem to hear. She could tell I wasn't able to hear what she was saying. She pulled me over to the side of the Reading Terminal and told me she was glad I'd called. Your parents will want to see me, too. I promised to come by the house—and to find Monte. "I want to see him first," I said. "Before I even go to the Rexford Circle pinball." My throat tightened again.

"Why'd you come back, Paul? Why really?"

"You think it's—"

"Charlene?"

"Yes, Charlene." You, Charlene, here everywhere I turn.

"Charlene, she—" The world all of a sudden seemed too vast and now Granny leaned in and I loved her as I loved you. "Maybe to restore something, to get back. Not as if anyone can go in reverse, or unwind the past. But Charlene had some terrible thoughts in the end. She became convinced—she became convinced that Monte was dead. That was one of them. She thought her brother had been killed in Vietnam," I finished.

"You told her—"

"Of course, I told her it wasn't true but I'll never know exactly when she lost consciousness or what she was thinking. Or what she believed." I had to admit to Granny the pain, Charlene.

Granny froze her expression. And what more? We stood at the top of the subway entrance. What more, Paul? Was it something about Monte? I turned and took her arm to help her down the stairs, an old lady in this vast world. This was enough for now. We took the number 10 trolley all the way to Lebanon Avenue and we hardly said a word. I walked her to your door and then, shyly begging off, I walked across the tracks, past my old house, and then, hesitating for a moment at the light, I waded in the traffic on City Line Avenue. My parents' new house was much farther than I thought, on foot. It was all the way at the end of the road.

2.

Paul Encounters Monte

Elsa Franklin Smith

I've seen Charles go through it and my own daughter Anita, though she never seems to change her expression, and now Paul. What I'm talking about is the moment of forgetting. I noticed it once, for just the slightest second, when he was sitting across from me in that dark restaurant in Chinatown. And this moment of forgetting makes you relive the sorrow again. This is how you know there's been some forgetting—because when it ends the face becomes drawn and loses color. This happens all of a sudden and you realize why and then you think back a minute and the person had seemed light again as they used to be, and unburdened. Paul lost his burden for just a minute in the Chinese restaurant and again today when he leapt up our steps like he used to and rang the bell.

Since I was sitting right there in the front window staring at the name on the piano—REGENT—at the letters of that word, which seemed so strange to me all of a sudden as if from a nonsense language, I heard someone outside, turned my head, saw his hand grab the rail as if he'd been racing down the street, like he used to, in love with my Charlene. I thought right then, as I eased myself up and unlatched the door, the poor boy is forgetting.

I sat him right down in the same chair by the window and brought him some iced tea. He looked funny at the iced tea and then he drank it down at once and put the glass to the side, on the napkin I'd handed him.

"Granny," he inquired, "you know where Monte is, where he hangs out?"

I hesitated. There are things I know because I know. But I can't always make an interpretation. I keep track. I don't tell anyone much because I can't be sure. What's Paul going to do, anyway? Go knocking on all the doors of Overbrook? Whatever Monte's up to, it might not be safe for Paul. Charlene would never forgive me.

"No, I don't really know, Paul," I said. "I see him leave, sometimes I know when he returns. Can't keep track of a grown man. But that can't be the only reason you came all the way over here, just to find out where Monte might be." I offered to get him some more iced tea. But, always polite, he went to the kitchen to get it himself. When he came back, and with a glass for me, I said, "Now let me ask you something," and I looked at the poor boy and noticed his beard coming in. He looked back at me with his heavy eyes, and I could see they were emerald, which I'd forgotten. "What did you mean when you said Charlene thought Monte had been killed? You reassured her, didn't you, you had to have promised her, Paul, you had to have promised her."

He turned away, took a sip of the iced tea, and put his hands on his knees. They gave me the feeling of square blocks, wooden blocks that produce nothing but a soft thud when you clap them together. That's how he was, Paul, unable to say anything more. And I knew by that he had more to say but couldn't. What was it? Something more about Charlene's last days? His own private business. But the business of this family is mine, and he's part of it. That boy is part of it.

"I came here to find him, Granny." So be it, Paul. "Then you better get comfortable, wait a while. I'll make you something to eat. He comes in late." Paul is slow to answer most of the time, but not then. "Tell me." He was almost begging. "I'm not sending you somewhere you best not go." Then I had an idea. "Could Monte work at your father's mill?" I had a vision that he got up every day and went there to make sweaters. (That mill was a little like a mythical place, like the toy factory in my father's dream.) Tell me. "You know Monte can draw, right? He can draw anything and he can just about fix anything, too. I gather he could be the one designing the newest line." He looked at me a long time. Did I surprise him? Truth is, I'd

16

been thinking this for a long time. Right up here I planned every detail of it. The Silk line could probably use some updating. When was the last time Charles got a Silk sweater for Christmas? It's been years! "But I don't know exactly," he said. "Forgive me I don't know. I don't even know what my father does. Is he is a businessman or a mobster?" The boy has a dry sense of humor. He's no mobster, Sam Silk! He laughed a little. I didn't know why. He sat back in the chair. Paul's hair is almost as thick as Negro hair. It makes you wonder. That family has its secrets, I gather, and realized I had forgotten. Charlene had been part of that family. It was hers, too, and one day she would have discovered the secrets right along with Paul.

"We all want to find Monte, Granny," he said. "I want to find him for Charlene. For obvious reasons."

"I know you do, Sonny."

"Where do I look?"

"I have a hunch or two," I said, "but don't you think he could find his way into that mill? Your daddy's a good man."

"You can point me, then? Nothing's going to happen to me. I think I know my way around these streets. Six years in Denver doesn't make the same kind of impression."

"Things have changed, Paul, don't fool yourself."

"Set me in one direction or the other."

I tried to avoid it, these hips aren't any good, but I took him upstairs and we went inside Jeanette's room in the back. She keeps it spotless. And she wasn't the one to go to Catholic school. We went to the window over her desk. Down there, on Lebanon. There's a boarded-up house. The look on my face must have changed, because he changed the tone of his voice, which had grown wistful, and airy, and he told me with love in his heart to keep a close watch over everyone. Then he brought his glass into the kitchen, washed it out, and left.

Paul Silk

I came down the steps from your house and turned the corner at the triangle. Right away, out of the corner of my eye, I spotted Monte. He was across the street, sitting on the second step of the corner house, at 62nd. I had the distinct feeling that he was talking to himself.

That block, remember together we called it "tawdry, which sounds like it should be somebody's name." What did Granny used to say? "You two have your own dialect, sometimes nobody else can understand it." One of the houses may have been boarded up. I recall those teenagers who liked to hang out on that corner, exactly where Monte was sitting, because they could drift up that block of 62nd and disappear in the loading dock of the store on the corner, the grubby supermarket. (We decided that Tawdry worked there, as a cashier.) When we spotted them we would quicken our pace, stiffen our shoulders, and hope to make it through. Immediately, I did as usual. I tensed up. Then I told myself it was only Monte. But was I ready to talk to him? I wasn't sure. I'd gone looking, but without thinking. Maybe not today. Maybe Granny had a point. Had he seen me? It wasn't likely. I should look straight ahead and keep going. But why so cowardly? Why couldn't I bear it? Yet I must have given myself away.

But then, as I kept watch out of the corner of my eye, he got up, turned in a circle, like a child playing a game of hide-and-seek, and came across to intercept me. Yes, this was Monte, smarter, sneakier, than anyone else. (It would be a challenge to keep him in any kind of job at the mill, but what was Granny talking about, having Monte design sweaters? Who designed them now?) He didn't say anything at first and I kept my hands in my pockets. Then, instead of a hug, maybe a handshake? I considered the idea as I felt warm and cold all over. He'd hardened, that was obvious and expected. I couldn't see his eyes; his sunglasses were mirrored. I decided not to beat around the bush. I told him there hadn't been a day in the past six years that I hadn't thought of him, often obsessively. "I want to help you," I said. And then I added, or rather, the unnecessary, insidious words slipped out, "when you're ready."

Do you know, Charlene, you would put your index finger to my lips to quiet me and joke that I'm like a drink that spills, slowly at first, as if in slow motion, and then all of a sudden all over the place. "You're spilling," you would say, you remember? Monte hardened again. Is this right: he went from dry clay to glazing oven, and out, rock-like. Then in his usual ironic voice, still with the echo of the fifteen-year-old boy I first met, he said some predictably awful thing to intimidate me into giving him whatever cash was in my pocket. I don't even want to say it, Charlene. He seemed desperate, his face oddly, for someone so obviously tense, slack.

Monte Johnson

Paul must have been at my house, again.

I was sitting on the stoop that leads up to the little porch at 6177 Lebanon and I saw him come around the corner. Hands in his pockets as usual. I waited until he got exactly halfway up the block. Then I got up, went behind the car parked in front of where I was sitting, and waited. Counted, with my eyes closed, to twenty. Opened them up, slipped on my sunglasses, and floated across the street. Then, at the other sidewalk, I stepped in front of him. The collar of my jacket flipped up and brushed my chin. That bothered me a little.

I let him (1) be scared because a tall blood had just come out of nowhere (you can marry a black woman but it's not like a nurse gives you a shot...I laughed at that...a no racism shot); (2) realize that beneath the drug dealer sunglasses it's me, old Monte, his brother-in-law ("my brother"), and (3) correct his expression, which went, in this order, from (a) oh fuck, this dealer's going to pull out a blade and I have no money in my pocket to hand him to (b) if there's one dude there's probably two, or three, they never act alone (and almost pee himself) to (c) Monte! to (d) Monte? No, wait, can't be Monte to (e) shit, it is Monte, oh my God, what is this world coming to? to (f) Monte, so good to see you, you need some help? You need anything? Let's get out of here, let's talk brother-to-brother. He put his stubby hand on my jacket sleeve and I tightened, not because I wanted to. I was done. I didn't care where he was coming from or where he was going to. But here is what I said instead of slipping out of his way:

Don't act like you know me.

Don't think I'm the same person you used to know. In other words, my brother, you don't know me.

Don't think you have any power in this situation.

I was taught to kill human beings, in war even medics can kill (I thought this but didn't say it out loud).

Give me whatever lousy dollar bills are in your pocket.

Stay away from my house.

And then, for some reason, I spit in his face.

Paul Silk

What exactly had just happened? Monte's spit was in my right eye and some of it got in my nose. For a minute, I tried not to breathe. I struggled to clean myself. I couldn't even find a leaf or a piece of Styrofoam cup. I used my shirt. The wind picked up. My eyelid stung from his saliva.

At the end of the block I found a pizza place. Only burning-hot water came out of the tap in the bathroom. I couldn't touch the water so I had to flick a tri-fold paper towel in and out of the water until it was wet enough and then let it cool. But the paper towel felt good on my face. I couldn't erase the image of Monte's cold, and frankly frigid, smile hesitating over me. How can I describe his disposition as I pressed the bills into his hand? Contempt? No, more like detachment, as if we didn't inhabit the same dimension. He made me absent. In the blur I saw him turn away. I saw the back of his leather jacket. He must have done something to lift it up and expose his skin just above the waist.

It would be better if I kept this image, of his skin, the real and absolute flesh of Monte, in my mind, and not his cold and disparaging look. But which was the real Monte, not of 1969 but 1976?

The spit that your brother launched out of his mouth, Charlene, it was meant to sting and humiliate. Was this the hate of generations mixed with fear and also sorrow? Was it meant for me, or you, or us together? I need to know. Did we wrong him, Charlene, did you abandon him on account of me. Did you die thinking he was already dead? Because he's alive. Oh, he's very much still alive. The streets of this city harbor a strange and disconsolate energy. It won't be any good if I let it twist me in a knot.

The girl behind the counter must have noticed I was in disarray. When I came out of the bathroom she asked if everything was OK. She had pimples on her forehead and dark, old-fashioned eyes. "I'm sorry, I have no money," I said. "Actually, I just got robbed." Immediately I regretted saying this, Charlene, to disparage him that way. The guy making the pizzas, presumably the girl's father, turned around. "Mugged? You want me to call the police, buddy? This damned city—Sit down, let me call the police. I could tell the second you walked in here something was wrong." What was to follow out of his mouth? Something hateful. But I didn't give him the chance. For various reasons, I told him that I didn't want to call the police. "You see how they've got it now, make people afraid to walk around the neighborhood. You want a slice of pizza?"

Monte Johnson

You probably think that after that I went inside the boarded-up house and got high. You'd be wrong (but I won't say why). I went and sat back down on the stoop, pushed my sunglasses to the top of my head, and had a look at the money Paul gave me, two crumpled up fives and four ones. Smoothed them out on my knee. Folded them in half and slid them inside the pocket of my jacket.

It's not like God came to me in that instant.

If human beings were smaller creatures, like mice or insects, we would have ant-sized seconds, minutes, and hours and, if the opposite was true, and we were the size of trees or giraffes, a second would be as long as a day, or maybe a week. I spit again and the spit went in an arc all the way out to the street. Just missed the shiny chrome bumper of the car.

A cop I've never seen before passed by and I spit a third time. Aimed right at the back of his heels. He stopped and said he wanted to know where I got the fourteen dollars (he could count just the same as me). He missed the thirty-nine dollars stuck inside my right sock.

"Can't loiter here," he told me.

"Can't God's creature?"

"I do the talking, faggot." (Had already tossed *If Beale Street Could Talk* to the gutter.)

"Charge me with sitting."

Fool. (I record a heavy desolation upon hearing that word, faggot, for some reason. For some reason. The same as but nakedly different from that feeling of Tu Do Street, Saigon. Back room on the right.)

I do what I got to do, which is to say: Get Silent. Wince.

"Get your filthy book from the filthy street." (Now look who can read.)

I had nothing to do so I walked up Wynnewood Road (I think) to the Overbrook School for the Blind. I stood behind a telephone pole so none of the students would see me.

The Overbrook School for the Blind is like the Alhambra Palace (jokers!). Who could have told me that?

Is he in his room? (No.) Is he on the streets? Is he in some drug house? Better not find him there. Maybe the cops picked him up. Rizzo's cops the same as (but nakedly different from) friendly fire.

Is he at the library? They never think to ask that.

The air turned cold when I walked up Woodbine. And some snow flurries were coming down when I got to 54th. The heat blew in my face the second I opened the door to the library. I sat in the window for a while with my arms crossed doing nothing. Got a drink from the water fountain. Pressed my pelvis up against the metal bar that makes the water come out and laid my mouth into the water like the football players and the shop heads did in school. And I gagged because the water came out so fast.

Paul Silk

The girl brought me a slice with pepperoni on a paper plate and a Coke. I told her I'd bring the money by later. The man told me he wouldn't think of taking my money. "Just come back another time with your friends."

The pizza was warm and good. The girl must have seen how quickly I'd eaten the slice because she came out from behind the counter again with another one, this time plain. And she brought over a glass shaker with red pepper flakes and another with garlic. I thought about the skin at the base of Monte's back and not the look in this face. I felt remorse for everything and at the same time a strange and unexpected hopefulness. I wanted the pizza man to survive, maybe fix up the place a little. His best customers are black, I felt surely, and one day he'll see the world for what it really is. With some latent instinct I reached inside my coat for a reporter's notebook. I could ask them a few questions. Are you father and daughter? Did your father open this place originally, or your grandfather? But it has been years, Charlene, since I carried a notebook.

Considerably better, I walked up 59th Street across the tracks and into Wynnefield. Here, 59th Street becomes 57th. Do you recall that? This was a detail I'd forgotten. Where did those two streets go?

And here, again, was Lebanon Avenue. At 54th Street someone called my name. It took a moment to recognize the voice; by the time I'd figured it out, there was Uncle Harry with a small bag of groceries. Aside from the funeral I hadn't seen him in years. "Look who fell from the sky," he said. He wore a cap and had whiskers growing out of his ears, his nose, his cheeks. After a few pleasantries, during which I promised to visit the next time I come up to see Nana, he asked, though he certainly knew the answer already, "So, you got a trade?"

I told him I was a journalist and that I'd be having an interview at the Inquirer, where I used to work. He looked at me as if he couldn't really remember and I had the feeling he was trying to come up with a joke. Instead, he said, "Did you see what the paper did to Rizzo?"

"The paper? Which paper?"

"Your paper. Somebody did a real number on him. A letter from the Mayor. Pretend. A fake letter. He doesn't talk to the press, so this was all made up. Made him look like he hates the Negro."

"Maybe he ought to talk to the press."

"They're only out to skewer him, put words in his mouth."

"I don't think he needs help with that."

"They make him into a bigot. His own driver is a black, a police officer just as he is."

"Doesn't mean he doesn't hate black people, I'm afraid."

"You might know," he said. "Listen…" Out came a joke about an Italian, a black, and a Jew inside an army tank. He offered me a cigar. He invited me to come up and play rummy. "Your grandmother isn't interested in playing anymore."

Monte Johnson

Now look what's on the table in the library window. (1) *Oreo* (oh shit); (2) Hammond World Atlas; (3) *Crime and Punishment*; (4) a sheet of foreign paper*, folded, stuck between number two (2) and number three (3).

Stuck, but sticking out.

You forgot? My arms are still folded. Medic Johnson, at ease! Nah. Don't worry, I ain't about to go fraggin'. At ease!

Yessir! (The arms of my eyes are still folded, if you get my drift.)

Experiment: Don't move yo' arms! Let 'em hang. And now close the eyes. Close them all the way, Medic. You got arms? No, sir. No arms, sir, just a torso, sir. Then you can't get the folded paper, can you? Well?

Well?

The fact of the matter, sir, is that I don't need to open the paper to know what's inside. That's in here.

Prove it.

I can prove to myself, inside myself. No further proof needed.

Prove it, Son.

Better I read it then.

With what arms, Medic? You can't read without arms.

I don't need to read it.

Why? You think you know it? Prove it. What's written on the page? Someone wrote you something? A spy message? Don't leave the spook hanging.

A beam from the black fish illuminates the army flashlight.
The frog in the mud is black too.
I wait until I see the light beam and stir the coffee.
Nothing dries under the banana tree.

I go to the well to keep the fish company.
The night moans, the light dims.

That's all it says?

It says everything.

Translate it. Interpret the code. Your brothers' lives depend on it. Hurry up!

That's it. Been translated already. I speak slow, sir. It's a song. One of them sing it to me. Then he write it down.** Then he feed me clean me fuck me. A man with skin the same color as ground-up peanuts, hair like coal.***

But what's it say, Medic? I can't understand the way these people speak.

*Paper made and used anywhere but the United States of America that is uniformly of flaccid, unsterile, unwhite, inferior, skinlike quality.

**The title of the song is "Medic Johnson."

***Tuan Van Sang, no age given. Killed in rescue of Medic Johnson from An Thanh.

3.

The Substance of Spit

Paul Silk

We were in your house, your parents' house on Columbia Avenue, near the triangle where Columbia crosses 63rd and Lebanon. What was the source of the strange and special feeling I always had crossing Lebanon Avenue, a feeling that began in childhood? There may have been a very specific source, a picture in a children's book of a camel or a bakery on 54th Street owned by "the Lebanese." To get to the Lebanese bakery we had to cross Lebanon Avenue, isn't that right? Or are my memories jumbled, the result of a child's confusion? Did I write a report on flags in the sixth grade, and was I drawn to the Lebanese flag because unlike the flags of other countries it displayed a tree, the cedar tree? Another image: an item printed on the Samuel Gompers School lunch menu: Lebanon bologna.

That word had to mean something. It was as real as the makeshift baseball diamond on Rexford Square, an extension of my house, my room. And you lived on this other part of Lebanon Avenue, across the tracks, in a different world, and now, Christmas 1968, I was in your house, sitting near the Christmas tree with silver tinsel, and Monte, tall and serious, with his finely chiseled face, and he was wearing a white turtleneck sweater. Monte was trying to tell you about the anti-war movement in his school, Overbrook High. He wasn't sure what he thought about it, marching and carrying signs. Usually so solicitous of your brother, on this night you couldn't keep focus on him because you had something you wanted to tell me. How quickly we were intimate, my dear Charlene. Was it because of Lebanon Avenue, as if an incipient, recurring memory? Even now, the street gives me a strange and special feeling. You demanded, "Monte, Monte, give us a minute," our hands in hands, and just then I saw a little mouse, the size and color of a river stone, peek out from under the radiator cover, and I didn't say a word. That's when you said you thought we should move, and you were worried about what I would say, and your eyes glistened more than usual. You said something about California. You wanted to move to a place "with a different history," you said, and you explained why. You didn't need to explain as we'd been discussing this issue for a while, since almost the beginning. I noticed, however, that you were becoming tense because you were worried about what I would think. The shape of your mouth had changed. For some reason, picking up on this in my subconscious, I said something stupid, like "everyone is the same."

You looked at me in such a way that all black people are forced to look at ignorant whites. "It's not the same for you. You can be anywhere."

Defiant for some reason, I said, "A Jew."

"An ugly Jew like you," you responded. And then you said, and you used the very word, "I have to get rid of this cancer."

"You're not making sense. You're not looking at the facts!" I insisted, unable to smother the primordial loyalty to my city, the greatest place in the world.

But you persisted, patiently, wading through my annoying subterfuge even then. Rizzo, you rightly predicted, would become Mayor. What would that mean? Exactly what's happened: black punishment for white failure, corruption, incompetence, and lies. And Charlene, it's only gotten worse. The police still have free reign and Rizzo uses them to punish political enemies. The Bicentennial, once supposed to be a world's fair, has been whittled down to a parade. You knew that if we stayed you would have endless material to report and make a name for yourself in your own city. But that wasn't enough to overcome the years of humiliation you were sure we would have to endure.

You'd forgotten about Monte, though he still sat there, with Dr.

King, the Overbrook anti-war committee, and your own father's (with such commanding influence) idiosyncratic patriotism on his mind, just to focus on me. Wasn't there something else, too? Something else he wanted to say, a reason he stared at you so long, something more personal. Monte had always confided in you and I was in the way. You were blind to it, Charlene, or were you afraid of what he might say? Was I—our future—a convenient excuse? What did Monte need to tell you? He was burning up to tell you something about himself.

"Denver. *The Denver Post*," you said. You were serious. You had done the research. Your eyes wouldn't detach from mine, shutting his out.

"What?" said Monte.

"Denver," you said, to me.

I said to myself, "White," because, of course, I thought of snow.

4.

Sam Silk Turns 57

Paul Silk

Maybe there is a faster way to go, but I drove through the old neighborhood. By missing the turn (twice) onto Overbrook Avenue, I found myself in front of my old house. I pulled over silently, leaned toward the passenger window, and gazed out at the red maple tree, and following the line of sight, the front door. The tips of the branches of the tree were like tiny flames. A cop walked by. I heard him before I saw him and then he was gone. I closed my eyes and let the sun penetrate and the footsteps grew fainter and fainter. A crack in the sidewalk near the front step, still unrepaired (you recall?), but the door was a new color, golden yellow. Finally, I pulled away.

Waiting for the light to change at Wynnefield Avenue, I decided I should go over to your house, 6147 West Columbia Avenue, and see if anyone wanted to come to celebrate my father's birthday. He had ordered enough bagels for the whole neighborhood. I should have turned left to go directly to the Lebanon Arms but instead I crossed Wynnefield Avenue, then Gainor and Diamond. Only a few seconds later, here was Lebanon. Your family has always been welcome at my parents' house. Who will I find at home on a Sunday at ten-thirty? Charles, surely. Granny? Anita? Jeanette? What could I say to Monte? Come have bagels and lox. Do you see your spit? It's still in my eye. And still it burns. I'll give you another fourteen dollars. And for that matter, come design my father's sweaters. And your older sister,

31

beloved older sister, when you returned from war, Monte, you found her everywhere in your house, everywhere and nowhere, and you can't forget a thing. The LeSabre's clock was meant to look old-fashioned. It had Roman numerals, but strangely elongated and curved to the shape of the dashboard it didn't appear the second hand could make the turn. I watched and waited at the corner of Lebanon Avenue. Turn left on 57th!, I could almost hear you say to me. Here was vast space, Charlene, as if the tracks that separated Wynnefield from Overbrook were a great and insurmountable chasm. Why hesitate now?

I knew, even as your "honorary Negro" (and you my "honorary Hebrew"), that the chasm was a mysterious force, race. And being mysterious, race had strange ways of erecting walls around itself that I'd lost practice breaking down.

Forgive me?

I fidgeted with the steering wheel and made a right onto Lebanon Avenue. A few minutes later, up the drive at the Lebanon Arms, I was helping my Nana Betty get into the front seat of the car. Harry slipped into the back seat, the must of his worn tweed jacket and the faint odor of cigar invading. "Have you heard the one about the," he started and I wasn't sure if I could let him go on.

I was disappointed in myself, frustrated at my complicity, and tortured all the same in the car that seemed, in the instant, my dear Charlene, a tiny shtetl.

Alan Silk

Karen spent too much time in the bathroom, which meant she was nervous about the brunch. I'm not sure why. It was just going to be another brunch, like all the others, with bagels and lox and cream cheese from Murray's Deli, and then a birthday cake for dad. I left the bedroom and went to check on the girls. Ann is seven and Beth is five. "We don't want to go, we're going to be the only kids. Can't we just stay here and play?" they said.

"How come we're the only kids? How come Uncle Paul doesn't have any kids?" asked Beth.

"Because Aunt Charlene is dead, stupid," said Ann.

"You said it's because a black-skinned lady can't get pregnant by a white boy, God says. But when are we gonna get cousins?"

"You're a liar."

"Both of you shut your mouths. Ann, if you ever—Go get dressed. Put on something nice or your grandmother will get on my case."

The wonders of progress. Now that they have aisles and shelves in the state liquor store you can browse as you wish. You used to have to know exactly what you wanted. No longer must you place your order with the man behind the glass. Browsing is how I found dad his present. I got him something even though my mother, when she called to tell me about the brunch, said, "Don't get him anything. He has everything he needs." At the state store I found him a Wild Turkey bottle shaped like a turkey, in porcelain, special edition. The head twists off. Now I had to find a bow to put around its neck.

When we got there the girls raced from the car as if the cage door had opened. Karen went right into the kitchen to see if my mother needed help. I'm not even sure she took off her coat. I went to say hello to dad in the other room. He had on a yellow sweater and white pants and was talking on the phone. The phone line in the study is the office line, Silk Industries. Who was he doing business with on a Sunday? I moved the kids out of the way and went upstairs in search of my brother. No one was there and so I went down to the kitchen and poured some coffee. My mother was cutting bagels. Bea, the housekeeper after all these years, was laying out the lox, the whitefish, and the sable onto trays. How much fish did they get? Karen was searching for serving forks, opening and closing drawers.

"Where's Paul?" I wondered.

"He went to pick up Harry and Nana." My mother put the knife down and took me into the hallway. "I didn't invite Charles and Anita. I just want you to know."

"So?"

"That's all. They live so close by and your father loves everyone. But if I invited them, I would have to invite Jeanette, Monte—"

"It doesn't matter." It was only brunch. "Does Paul care?"

33

"I'm not sure he's even realized. He didn't even seem to know about the brunch until he got up this morning."

I shrugged. My brother the newspaperman is the last to know.

"I just wanted you to know," she said again. "That's all." Then she paused and I waited because I knew there was more. "It's better for him this way. He has to move on."

Harriett Silk

The mountain of bagels—Sam had ordered two dozen of them—took its place on the dining room table as if it was Polyphemus's island. I'll end up freezing half of them, which is why I insisted on being the one to cut them. No sense cutting more than we need today. I gave Karen a red onion and instructed her to slice it thin. I'm sure I said "thin" ten times. Though she just looked at me. I might have asked her to explain why Odysseus should have dared enter the cave of the Cyclops.

This was Sam's day, my husband's fifty-seventh birthday celebration (his actual birthday had been a few days before), and the fish, from Murray's, the lox actually sliced thin, and the sable, with its pearlescent flesh and copper skin deepened with paprika, was a satisfying sight. I think perhaps only Alan understands the intricate nature of these family gatherings. Mother will make an immediate effort to sit with Betty even though they have little in common aside from their age. They used to have a mutual understanding and both of them probably thought they got the upper hand. Betty would compliment my mother on her ring or necklace and in this way demonstrate her own good taste. Simone would ask Betty about something important to her. Needlepoint, for example. She purposely never asked about Abe. She wanted Betty to speak for herself.

Now, of course, Betty is going senile. She can't hold a conversation. She isn't quite sure where she is. Mother will only last so long and then she'll move on to Harry, who at least will tell her an off-color joke. But Harry sometimes sounds like a lunatic. If he shows up, my brother, Albert, the lawyer, will relieve her of these obligations to Sam's side of the family and if he doesn't (he hasn't yet arrived), mother is likely to corner Paul, an intellectual like she is, and both have been journalists, and force him to discuss politics. (For my money, Paul is, however, as much a Silk as a Birnbaum. He slides through life as his father does.) She'll talk Paul's ears off about Rizzo, and if, at first, he doesn't seem interested, she'll find another way. Mother hasn't come to our house, in case it isn't obvious, with genuine affection for Sam. He's tried to win her over, as Sam enjoys almost any type of person, but he's never been able to overcome almost insurmountable odds: (a) that he comes from a family of Russian Jews, "right out of the shtetl" (mother's prejudices might surprise the casual observer who doesn't know better); (b) that he seduced her eldest child, who chose him over any number of members of the Cornell University class of 1938 (or, for that matter, '37 or '39), including the famous anthropologist Linus Etting; (c) that he trapped this child into marriage by impregnating her before proposing. "Trapped," it should be noted, is mother's term for choice. I find it imprecise and frankly a little hysterical.

Paul Silk

I played with those two girls you liked to call "my bright nieces." They attacked me from behind when I wasn't looking and dragged me to the floor. And, after Alan presented my father with a special ceramic edition bottle of Wild Turkey in the shape of a wild turkey (I had hoped the whiskey poured out of the turkey's beak, but this wasn't the case—the head twists off instead), the girls insisted on playing turkey the rest of the afternoon, claiming that it was actually Thanksgiving.

I watched my father, Sam Silk, now fifty-seven years old, and I wondered who he was. He sat in the same chair the entire day with his drink and the occasional plate of smoked fish and then the cake that was presented to him, which caused the girls to jump into his lap and blow out the candles.

But who is this man, and what exactly is the nature of his business? All of a sudden I had no idea what he wanted from life. He seemed only a worn out, self-destructive Russian Jew. You never could understand when I would say, in response to something, "but that is the German part of me speaking," or "that's the tragic Russian." You didn't see the point in tracing a person's character in this way, though secretly did it fascinate you? And you would say, "Paul, how many generations has it been? Weren't they all Jews, descended from the same people?" We might diverge then into a discussion exploring the debate between nature and nurture and you the practical one arguing, "of course it's both." But I would sit there pained, because I wanted you to know that German Jews became German, perhaps more German than the Germans, more idealistic, rigid, and rational, and the Russian Jews more Russian than the Russians, and therefore corrupt, emotional, melancholic, and conspiratorial, and what they shared as Jews, combativeness and righteousness both (and sorrow), made it difficult to inhabit the same world. And, my dear Charlene, I was both, couldn't you see?

I was made from both, but how and in what ways? "But you are who you are," you would say, and I would tear up, just as I may now. Can you taste the tears across the impossible distance?

Simone (German, as surely you recall) found me sitting on the piano bench with a bagel piled high with fish—you've seen this, you know already—the onion falling to the floor, the California olive rolling around on my plate, cream cheese in my eye. She magically appeared and sat down on the ottoman next to me. The woman is both wrinkled and elegant. For once I could feel her next to me, like a real grandmother. I could even hear her breathing, Charlene. Has her face, her cheeks, her eyes, always been so weathered? Yes, yes, she really lived. And she is living still, trying to save the world. No, not save the world. She is simply offended by Rizzo's harsh stupidity, his inelegance, his violent nature. The city is on a precipice and he is about to shove it over the edge. She wanted to tell me about the meeting she had attended at a church on Germantown Avenue about Rizzo and what to do about him. She had to tell me about the woman running the meeting, a "captivating and brilliant woman," and "not whatsoever naïve." Why did I have a feeling she was thinking of you? I chewed my bagel and she laid out the case for a vote to recall

Rizzo, which seems to me an impossible thing to do. All this time Uncle Harry had been listening. Half the Silk side of the family is from Odessa, like Isaac Babel. They're Russian. More Russian than the Russians. They'll curse and say anything, you see?

"Rizzo saw the way the world was being ruined for the little people," said Harry, trying to provoke Simone. "That's all this is."

"The little people," Simone said. "They are smarter than you think."

She got up then, and walked away. And Harry, always the jokester, sat down, turned around, opened the piano, and began to play "The Marseillaise."

I'm exhausted. Tomorrow I will go to the Inquirer for an "informal interview." Why do I ramble on? Because I'm filled with remorse, my dear Charlene. I turned back on 57th Street. I turned back from your daddy and your mama, from Jeanette and Monte and Granny. I turned back. They weren't there for my father's fifty-seventh birthday. I could easily have picked them up. I fear holding on and I fear letting go.

5.

Haunted in the Night

Paul Silk

I had just turned twenty, and I was drifting at the edge of the swelling crowd. Any minute, we were told, any minute. Should I have been inside the crowd? That's something we would talk about later, much later. No, I was happy with the six or seven interviews I'd gotten already. You asked me what I was doing, remember? You came up to me, the same angled cheekbones that drew everything about you to your lips. You wore a hair band. It was the third of August, florid.

"You going to write down what he says?"

I looked at the reporter's notebook in my hand, felt for the pencil behind my ear. Did I think you were about to grab it, Charlene? "So far I'm more interested in what all these people have to say."

"Which is what?"

"Depends. Everyone says something different."

"Give me an example," you insisted.

I stuttered, shuffled pages.

"That," you pointed.

"What?"

You grabbed the notebook. "Here. You wrote, if I am making this out correctly, 'He is ours.' What's that supposed to mean? That man doesn't belong to you or me or anyone."

"I think she means he's a symbol, an icon, a hero."

"Old or young?" you asked.

"Who?"

"The lady who told you that."

"Middle."

"You think that's fair? Anyway, Dr. King is everyone's hero or no one's."

"You assume—"

"Am I wrong?" you demanded.

"All the same."

"Hey," you said, "hey now." People kept shoving by but you didn't care. I can still hear the crowd buzz turn into song. *This little light of mine, I'm gonna let it shine…*

"Hold on." The singing stopped and people had started clapping. "He's coming on."

That was our first conversation, up against the doorway of a storefront church left half ajar, with an old, three-legged chair to keep it open. I wore a dark blazer and a dark tie, and hi-tops. You found people for me to interview once the program was over. You told me what to ask them, remember? Is Dr. King's philosophy of non-violence right for us here in Philadelphia? Or do you think other measures are needed to counter the police? Do you plan to join the fight now? Do you think any judge will break a white man's will? At issue was the desegregation of Girard College, Stephen Girard's will that kept black boys out of the school. You stood next to me, so sure of yourself. You said, "We're out here taking the pulse." You already knew how. You said you had to wait until the crowd dissipated and they let the trolleys through. You were on your way to the university for freshman orientation. I had to get back to 30th Street Station.

We sat at the rear of the trolley. You paged through my notebook, laughing at my handwriting. You were eighteen, Charlene. You never made it to thirty.

"You afraid of the draft?"

Did I say I hadn't thought about it? Did I look past you, out the window? You were prescient, somehow. The draft call had only just begun, but maybe you had heard people in your neighborhood were getting called. I suppose I mentioned a post-graduate fellowship. The Ford Foundation was offering grants to young journalists. I had a year to go.

"See that," I said, as we approached the 36th Street turn. "Over there. The world's first soda fountain."

"Where? I've been coming this way all my life."

"That right there."

"I don't think so."

"No, really." Why did I insist? What came over me? You didn't believe me, anyway.

The trolley dipped into the tunnel, into darkness, and that's when our life together began. Or that was the prologue. I didn't see you for two years. Or rather you spotted me. And later, Charlene, we had all the light, didn't we? Snow on the ground increases ultraviolet light by eighty percent. You found that out right away when we moved to Denver. You asked the editor if anyone had investigated this subject and he shrugged, as if the newsroom was a cave and we were all cavepeople. You didn't want us to be cavepeople. Not you and me. You insisted we wear our sunglasses all year long.

The darkness now, Charlene, it's everywhere. Eleven years later. Here on this side, and yours? Those last days, what am I supposed to do with them? Weeks and months later I can't excise them. You, of all people, confused. You, of all people, having lost your mind. It was the cancer or it was the morphine. It wasn't you. I had to tell myself it wasn't you. The cancer or the morphine robbed you and left you caved in and confused. It made you betray yourself at the end, Charlene, so that it wasn't even you. So I tell myself ten thousand times a day.

"Why did you let me do it," you asked, your hand like a marionette lifted up above the bed sheet and then dropped, the puppeteer careless, or maybe new, a puppeteer in training. You winced. I didn't. I didn't know what you meant.

I closed my eyes and tried to warm your hands in mine. When I opened my eyes now yours were closed. You'd fallen asleep. I put your hands under the sheet. No! I couldn't take it. I moved your hands, one at a time, out from under the sheet. And I held them again to keep them warm. I told myself never to take my eyes away. A little while later you started speaking. Your voice like Granny's best hot grits, only sharper, there is something otherworldly about those grits even without the bacon fat you made her remove, even Granny's grits had to be vegetarian. All the way to the end even fainter and fainter your voice stayed the same. That's worst of all, the words and the voice became misaligned.

I bent down. Your voice was the same, but you couldn't project it. Your lips were cracked. Damn it. "Monte…" I couldn't quite hear.

"Monte?"

"Monte's funeral, we should never have missed Monte's funeral. I mean the memorial, there was no proper funeral. Because they couldn't find him. A whole army and they couldn't find him."

"Shhh."

"Daddy thinks he was taken prisoner, but I know he's gone. He's not coming back. They had the memorial but we didn't go. We couldn't go. We couldn't get the plane."

"But Monte came home. You saw him. We saw him, Charlene, in Philadelphia. He came home. He's alive."

You closed your eyes.

"Charlene, your brother is fine! We'll call and talk to him later, Charlene, after you rest." And then I tried to change the subject. *Black Sunday* had just come out and I'd assigned someone to review it for the Sunday book section. I had the draft of the review with me. I was going to edit it while you slept. I started to tell you about the novel. The main character haunted by Vietnam and I must have compounded your confusion, if you could hear at all. I stopped myself short, closed my eyes, leaned in and listened to your breathing. I listened for hours, all that night and the next morning. You never spoke again, Charlene. We never spoke again.

Harriett Silk

I've been a teacher for almost forty years. Young people act out their feelings. Even the quiet ones need to excise something. We've all read newspaper stories about the atrocities of Vietnam. We've seen it on *60 Minutes*. I don't know what exactly Monte went through. He was a medic. War must have terrified him, a sensitive boy.

Sam snores away and the new clock radio reads 2:47.

Still no one I've had in the ninth or tenth grade compares to Monte Johnson. He loved to read; he would note the double—and, to his own glee, triple-entendre—before any of the others in the class had grasped the basic meaning of the text. And he would explain it to them, not without a slight condescension, and they would listen. Probably some sneered. Monte kept himself a bit separate from the rest, but not in a disadvantageous fashion. Of course, he had his sister, who hadn't been a pupil of mine since she attended parochial school. She practically raised him. I didn't understand any of that the way I would come to later. He was a born iconoclast. Adored his sister but refused to follow her to parochial high school. He had an impulse and an insight far beyond his years. What put Monte in my head? The mind gallops in these dark hours. My son is a widower. This came to me at 3:07 with a spiteful force.

Paul Silk

No, Charlene, I'm not talking to you—I can't. I don't want you to hear me thinking to myself, I'm trying to get away. Tell me it isn't wrong—no, I don't need you to tell me it isn't wrong. But you are everywhere on Lebanon Avenue. In the worn upholstered chair where I sat drinking iced tea with Granny, at the kitchen sink. This is you I had tried to leave in Colorado. It isn't cruel to say it, but why did I come home? You laughed this city away and we turned our backs and we hid, for five years we hid in Denver, but in reality you're still here, this city in you and you in it. You needed to leave because you couldn't escape it. The cancer inside you was the cancer of Lebanon Avenue. And what am I doing back here? Reversing time? Even here in this strange house. Your things are right over there. Your earthen smell, Charlene, your visage in Granny's, the night of your confusion. The night you left me.

Now Monte's trapped me in his hot and unctuous spit. And shriveled me so I don't know what I want or how to think. You're a literalist, Paul, you would say. I would say, so are you. No, you're wrong, you would reply, I like real things, only real things matter. You, you take everything said as real. To love me forever. To love you forever. Forever is a literal word. I'd never let a writer use it in the newspaper. It's an impossible word, has no place in a journalist's lexicon.

To keep you close by I think I need to let your brother go. You understand? I need to be free. He's trapped me, even if, Charlene, the spit was intended for you. It reached my bones, I want you to know. It's settled there. I can feel it burning in the dark of night.

6.

Jeanette Has Something to Ask

Jeanette Johnson

Hold on! Was that just Paul, Charlene's Paul, getting on the El as I was getting off? Wearing that ugly old peacoat? His hair practically an afro! And a beard, too. I get excited when I see the crowds of people coming on and off the car, people weaving into each other like fabric strings, that's what it would look like if I could see it from above. Some times of day all the strings are parochial school girls in their pleated skirts criss-crossing with freaks from the university. I get a feeling in the pit of my stomach when I see the girls from Hallahan or West because my sister wore that uniform and they remind me of her and at the same time I'm glad I never had to. Good thing Monte said no way he was going to Catholic school because if he hadn't done that I would have had to and I was always afraid of getting whacked by the ruler. What I like about coming down here is that everyone is going in a different direction. You can get bunched up in it, like what happened just now when I saw Paul out of the corner of my eye. I yelled, "Paul! Paul! Turn around!" but he didn't hear me, because we were bunched up, like the strings were tangled. But the best thing is when you break through. Then people start crossing in front of you sideways. I like the feeling of gliding through those people rushing to the subway and I'm singing in my head, "That's the way I like it (uh-huh, uh-huh)," and depending on how big those crowds are I'll go up staircase number two, three, or four.

My friend Trish won't even go into Center City with me because she doesn't want all those people in her space, but I think she's just too afraid. I don't see why anyone would stay all the time in Overbrook, where everything is always the same. Down here I can walk for hours and never see the same thing twice. I talk to people. The freaks in Rittenhouse Square are the easiest to talk to. Although I always say no when they offer me a drag of their marijuana cigarette. They don't know what to make of me. But I like the way they look at me, not like other white people. They keep going on, "Grow your afro, grow your afro, it's who you are!" One of them took me to the Gilded Cage and we were eating some sweet bread and drinking pineapple nectar and one of them said, "Let's go for belly dancing" and another, "You got to come with us to the Lebanese place." I can't lie, I was truly nervous. But I said to myself, "I'm not missing this." We walked for a long time on streets I never seen and one of them said we were crossing the border into another country. I didn't know what he meant, but we just kept going, arm-in-arm, three of us arm-in-arm, and me in the middle. When we got there the place was small and mostly empty and the owner, he has big ears, took my hand and said how glad he was to see me, as if I'd ever seen him before. Everything smelled like garlic. Someone said the dancing happens upstairs and I didn't know if we were the ones dancing or if there was a kind of show. The owner told us to sit and he asked us if we were hungry. I guess the walk made us hungry.

A few minutes went by. The whole thing had made me light-headed because everything was new, and I just sat quiet and looked at my hands and then the tables and the faces of my friends. Everything sped up and then it slowed down. Trish would have run out of there, but then she wouldn't have had any idea how to get back home. Then the owner brought out the food, chicken and flat bread, called pita, and salad. And a whole bunch of plates with pretty flowers on them and strange things I had never seen, not even at a party at the Silks'.

I thought we were going to eat then leave because no one mentioned dancing again. I wasn't sure. The man with those big ears came out with a silver pitcher with little cups and poured us some coffee.

"I made it extra sweet," the owner said, and he poured it from way up above the table and you could see the coffee drawing a line in the air. The whole time he did that he never took his eyes off me. So I looked down to see if he missed or spilled. He never did, not even a drop. I almost clapped.

Now we're going to leave, I thought, and I started to think if I could get the subway from there and take the 10 trolley home. But then one of my friends said it was time and we went upstairs through red and purple and blue and green beads into a red room. I didn't see him at first but someone was playing a guitar and someone else drums, but not normal drums, a box he was sitting on and banging it between his legs, and three girls, one with brown hair and one blonde, with heavy eye make-up, and one in a black dress, one in a purple dress, and one in a green dress, with sequins, and their bellies exposed. They were belly dancing. One of the freaks kissed me (I wasn't surprised), but I wanted to watch the dancers. I couldn't take my eyes off them, their bellies, the way they seemed to twist from the inside. The room filled up. I think I was in a trance. I got off the trolley late that night and I looked up at the street sign that said Lebanon Ave. and I got a strange feeling again in my stomach.

Since my sister died a voice came inside my head and said that I was supposed to continue living her life, except that we are so different it didn't make any sense. But when I'm walking around Center City I'm always looking for mixed couples, and usually it's a black guy, and he's usually tall, not sure why that is, but it is, and a white girl (once I saw a black guy and a little Chinese girl and they seemed so happy and normal). I guess there's not that many black girls like my sister who find a white guy to love. But Paul is Jewish, I think that's why. I walk down to Chestnut Street and sometimes I go on South Street and then down to Penn's Landing and when I go there I read all the signs about the first things to happen in Philadelphia and I feel a pride come up. I look at the people more than the buildings and especially when I see a mixed couple I feel like this is my city. I get shivers up my spine. Unlike my sister, I want to stay here. But somehow I also know that Frank Rizzo, the mayor, would do anything he could to keep me worried all the time. He's a bully. That's when I get a little afraid for myself, but really scared for Monte.

Paul is back in town and nobody told me? Maybe he can help. I need to talk to him, but I'm nervous, because if I hear the sound of his voice I might start to cry. I need to ask him some advice.

He's smart, just like my sister—and I don't mean smart like Monte, smart for no good reason—that's why they ended up together married. I need to ask him something. My sister Charlene didn't make a will. She didn't. For someone so smart that was pretty dumb. When I get a real job, and if I get married, I'm making a will. What I want to ask Paul is if I could have that turquoise ring of hers. I could wear it every day to remember her. Also, that color is really in. That's not the real reason, just something extra. I wonder where Paul is staying. At his parents' new house? I'm not even sure where that is. What I want to know is, has he kept all of my sister's things?

7.

Seeking Sam Silk

Paul Silk

I could have called my father and asked if Eddie could pick me up, but that seemed presumptuous and for some reason dangerous. But I had to be at the Inquirer building at Broad and Callowhill at ten. I couldn't fathom driving. Even picking up my grandmother and Harry had made me uneasy. I tried to recall the bus lines—you always knew them like the back of your hand, simply a matter of your competence. Where were the stops? Which bus did I take when I was fifteen or sixteen? (This you couldn't know.) The G? The G went down 56th Street, where you could catch the El on Market Street. Did it run from Wynnefield on 54th? This seems right. But from here, in the suburbs, I'd have to walk down there, and that walk, I now understood, takes almost an hour. There was another bus, or was it a trolley? The 40? I have a distinct memory of an endless ride, uncomfortable seats, everything bunched up, and, like the car that became my own shtetl, a tortured and parallel world, out of time. The bus had its own smell, language, and rules. Are there buses in the suburbs? I forgot to ask. A train? I had heard that a government train line, Conrail, had taken over the commuter lines. Was there a station nearby?

The phone book was in a drawer in the kitchen. Here was a map of the Penn-Central and another of the Reading before they were put together into Conrail. There didn't seem to be a Conrail map. Where was I, exactly? The phone book could answer this question. The entire county was spread across several pages and some of the streets of the city, along the borders, in gray shading instead of white. I had to get dressed, I had to put my things together in my leather case. Here was my parent's street, Cornell Road, the first time I'd seen it on a map. So close to the river, but you'd never know it. The "Hidden River." The Manayunk station on the Reading line, now Conrail, was very close by. I could walk over the bridge at Belmont Avenue. The problem was that past my parents' house Cornell curved around to another suburban street, in a closed loop. It didn't connect. I'd have to walk a half-mile in the opposite direction and then I'd have an even longer walk along Rock Hill Road. Or I could cut across the fields.

An hour later I was on an old train that must have been built in the 1930s. The lights flickered. The vinyl seats were loose and worn. I'd found a station. The Cynwyd Line, once a stop on the Pennsylvania Railroad. It served my parents' suburb.

When I was a cub reporter I liked to talk to the clerks in City Hall, listen to their family stories. They talked about their grandparents more than their own kids, and they would reveal which other clerk was cheating the system and usually this meant they were too. Each time I changed assignments it was because a new editor had been hired. A lot of the old guys retired when we were there and now the paper was completely different. Walter Annenberg sold the paper to the Knight family of Miami before he became Ambassador to England. Now the paper was aggressive in pursuit of corruption, police brutality, Frank Rizzo. Did they need another features editor? Almost six years an editor at *The Denver Post*. Would I have to prove myself again?

The train came into Suburban Station only a few blocks from the paper. I turned up the collar of my coat as I walked up Broad Street, with the strange feeling of being detached, as if the city was receding behind me in the background, but at the same time the paper was getting farther and farther away. I'd never noticed before the slight incline of Broad Street as it led north.

At Callowhill, finally, I felt a tinge of nerves, a lightness in my stomach, a hot flash. They won't hire me to be an editor. I tried to imagine reporting again. I hated reporting, forcing people to reveal what they don't want to, what they would be better off keeping to themselves. You always said that wasn't true, that no one tells you something they don't want to. The stories were out there, but "they don't exist without the journalist." A rhyme. Our rhyme. The reporter sorts them out, double-checks them, and makes sure they have a beginning, middle, and end. In Denver, where the people are friendlier and also a bit self-satisfied (having conquered the West), I don't recall you ever worrying that a source was afraid to confront reality. Perhaps reality wasn't so frightening as it is here, where it must be twisted for the sake of survival.

I could edit, Charlene. For us, editing meant editing out Philadelphia.

The crowd in front of the massive newspaper building, our "tower of truth," snapped me out of it. Mostly men, some with signs. I didn't attempt to read them. I didn't want to be late for the interview. So I slid through, a skill I'd learned on the subway as a kid. "Silk always gets through!" My father used to sneak into the movies this way and I had learned it from him without even realizing. Is this how we learn, become ourselves, through osmosis? But I didn't want to be Sam Silk. I never did. I wanted to do something important and I found the newsroom. And you, Charlene, I found you.

Someone grabbed me by the shoulder with such force that I guessed there had to be a fire (thus the crowd mounded on the sidewalk) or someone dangerous let loose in the newsroom, upstairs, out to settle a score. "No one's going in there!"

"But why?" I was nearly shouting to be heard.

"Sorry mister, no one's going in and no one's coming out."

"I have an interview, I have to be there. There's no fire!" I grabbed the door handle trying to remember the floor I was to go to when another arm, in a black leather jacket that felt cold against my neck, hooked me backwards. My satchel slipped off my shoulder to the ground and I lost my balance. I jammed my wrist to break the fall and still I had no idea what was going on. No one asked if I was OK. Then someone: "Look, buddy, this is a labor action against the paper. During a labor action, you do what we say." Really, who says so? But I must not have said anything. "We're shutting the paper down." I didn't recall the paper having too many labor issues. The Teamsters, who ran the delivery trucks, could cause trouble, but I was sure I'd seen the carpenter's patch, maybe one from the steamfitters, the sheet metal workers. This was some kind of unilateral "action."

At the edge of the crowd I recognized a photo editor—you probably didn't know him. He didn't remember my name. The man had trouble breathing. He huffed and puffed standing still, one hand on a basketball belly. The wind blew around his matted hair, lifted up like the feathers of a lost or dying bird. I asked him if he'd been able to get inside earlier. "I tried to get in the back, off the parking lot, but they've barred the door. Same with the loading dock." He squeezed out all the air he could. It was impossible to picture him climbing up the loading dock.

"I'm not sure I understand what this is about," I said. I buttoned my coat. I told him about the interview.

"You don't know? I had figured—" He gave me the impression of having spaghetti in his mouth. "Rizzo. He's ordered all these union guys to close the paper, block the presses. He took offense at something we published. He didn't get it was satire." The photo editor made a face as if to say, "Not too smart."

"How do we know—how can we be sure—the Mayor ordered this?" Was this real?

"Fingerprints—" the photo editor started to say. "He learned from Nixon. Thinks the press is the 'enemy of the people.'"

Now I noticed police lights flashing along the sidewalk edge. The cops were in on it, too. Fingerprints. I started to walk away and the photo editor turned and caught my attention. "Try calling tomorrow," he said. "It's not like he can stop the presses forever." I'd forgotten about the dour wit of oldtimers. Probably nothing fazed them.

The sun must have moved behind City Hall tower; March cold slapped my face. It wasn't the tower, but clouds that in their architecture made it seem the city was ringed by snow-capped peaks. This couldn't be a city of mountains. It was incapable of floating.

Men downtown in suits and trench coats, tweed manteaux, fedoras, Italian caps, burly satin jackets with warm stuffing, leather and fringe, sideburns, beards, mustaches, heavy eye glasses, even a pince-nez, in this city that deadens time, and traps it so that anyone, depending on taste, social status, bank account, race, or age, can pass through the decade of his choosing. An earthly kind of fantasy. Now is eternally suspect, eternally forced to justify itself. Maybe not in this Bicentennial year, or maybe more so. The anniversary demands a gaze back to another time.

Maybe that is it, exactly why we had to leave.

I sat on the edge of a stone planter in City Hall courtyard. They no longer bring prisoners in here on buses painted the city colors of cornflower and maize and because of that, even despite the chill, you can sit and gaze at whoever walks by. Does my father ever come down here on business? Perhaps to meet with Uncle Albert, his lawyer, perhaps for a drink with an out-of-town client. No, Charlene, Sam Silk isn't a lawyer or a banker, an intellectual, or even a working man, a pipefitter, a fan of the Eagles or the Flyers; his hands are smooth though he has no college degree; he isn't religious, or liberal, or close-minded. He isn't exactly open-minded, either.

He walked into the suburbs (with blind intent, marching), with one word on his lips, "privacy."

I got up from my spot, purchased a soft pretzel with mustard from a street vendor whose eyeglasses were taped together at the bridge, enough tape to hold together any real bridge or street or neighborhood, and I walked back up Broad Street to Callowhill, the pain in my wrist subsiding; perhaps the blockade had ended. But when I saw police in a line to protect the Mayor's union henchmen and not the right of freedom of the press, I turned back around. Back at City Hall I went down to the underground concourse, purchased some subway tokens, and slipped through the crowd onto the eastbound platform. A few minutes later, the train, up out of the tunnel, was hurtling toward Kensington, home of Silk Industries.

Paul Silk

The El speaks its own secret language; the stops, like the narrow width of the streets of the city, aren't very far apart. From City Hall station, it's only two blocks to the next stop, 13th, and two blocks to the one after that, 11th. Then three to 8th and three more to 5th, 2nd, and with each stop in this direction the color of the passengers' skin becomes whiter and whiter.

The train emerged from under the Benjamin Franklin Bridge, my forehead resting against the window. Around the time my grandfather, Abe, turned fifteen, his father, Shmuel, one of the only educated Jewish men from his village, purchased the Glossheim Woolen Mill at Emerald and Dauphin Streets in Kensington and renamed it Silk Industries. Shmuel decided to pass the mill, which he had added onto considerably, to his sons, Abe and Harry, desiring that both of them join the business. It's never been clear to me what happened, but Abe ended up with the mill and he, in turn, handed it off to my father, Sam. But my father hasn't ever discussed his plans for Silk Industries. Has he secretly offered it to Alan, after all a businessman? Does he have plans to sell? Why isn't there a succession plan? Why haven't there been any family discussions? Why do I know so little about the business, the products, the employees? You often asked, not because you cared how wealthy my family was, but because you were maddened that I didn't know. These questions, like an invisible hand, seemed to press me down the stairs at York-Dauphin station. Now I wanted answers. And I thought to myself, "Who was the Petit Dauphin? Was he also the Sun King?"

Louis Turner

Today Eddie didn't assign me any deliveries and so when the boss's son showed up, I was sweeping the floor in the main office. The old linoleum is crumbling in the corners where the adhesive gave out. All the dirt and dust collects there and nobody but Louis can get it clean.

I lit a cigarette right before Junior came in. I showed him in to see Crazy Eddie in the office next door to the boss's. Junior looked surprised to see Eddie occupying the office. OPERATIONS MANAGER, it says, in gold, on the frosted window of the door. Instead of going back to the front office, I stood in the corner. Did Mr. Eddie want me to take the visitor around? He was all right, this one, knows a good-looking lady when he sees one, Rest In Peace. "Better to take him in to see Mr. Silk," said Eddie. Crazy Eddie didn't have much more to say.

The boss was eating a sandwich at his desk. Eddie keeps his office as he keeps the Mercedes: clean and polished. I been inside messier funeral homes. But never seen the top of the boss's desk. The second time, now, I hung back, awaiting further instructions. The old radiator was gurgling like somebody had his hands around its neck squeezing hard. Mr. Silk is usually friendly, but I had a hunch why he stayed sitting there a minute. I thought I had it figured out when the boss got up, made a noise of surprise and came around his desk. Gave Junior a hug. I got a tear in my eye. Louis don't make this shit up. Boss got out the new sweater, the one for Conrail with the zipper that don't work. That had to be sent back five times until it did. But that's Crazy Eddie, Mr. Quality Control. I had to get out of there. Couldn't watch. I went back to my desk, got out the map, checked all the dots. Darn near everything on that map. Before I know it, I'm hearing the boss's footsteps, his loafers snapping against the floor and Young Buck shuffling. Couldn't have been a whole minute. Boss is pushing Young Buck out the door. "Let's go around the corner and have a drink." Boss don't miss an opportunity. I had to laugh. That dog had him out the office before I could light up again.

Sam Silk

Paul came into the office right behind Louis. This was the kid who crept into my office to ask what else he should do now that the filing, or whatever I'd given him to do for twenty-five cents an hour, was done. He'd come in laughing and fooling and he made you want to laugh and fool with him. Now he's come for something. There's always a reason. I brought out samples of the new cardigan sweater, in navy and heather gray, Silk Industries was about to produce for the new railroad, Conrail. Ticket agents, engineers, conductors—all of them are going to wear this sweater, with the Conrail logo embroidered on it. Right away Paul took off his coat, grabbed the sweater from me, and tried it on. He tugged at it, zippered it right up. Naturally, I fixed the sleeves. He had them all tangled up. What did he think? This was the spring model, light, with nylon and polyester. Only five percent wool. And to do it I'd had to retrofit a dozen knitting machines. Did he like it? I couldn't tell. He didn't look comfortable. The sweater fit him fine. Was this the latest fashion, he wanted to know. Like, what? Vogue? Railroad Enthusiast? What did he mean by that? The sweater was old-fashioned? Of all the fool things. He doesn't know a damn thing about business. I had half a sandwich on my desk and now I had a mind to finish it. Then I looked at my sandwich and I looked at the kid. I unclenched my fist and I said let's go around the corner and have a drink. Louis was back in his office staring at the map. He brings that thing out so I will see it. Some day I'm going to take a match to it. I ordered him to shut the door.

We sat right down in my usual spot, to the left of the door. I've known the barkeep since he was a teenager bussing the tables, as good a relic of Kensington as any Jacquard loom. He came over, and I introduced him to Paul. This is the one who got away. This is what they look like out west. The barkeep asked him what kind of work he does. Paul was smart enough to say he was between jobs, and leave it like that. In Kensington, they don't like college professors and they don't like journalists. I'm not sure which they think is worst. My son with his bushy hair and beard could be either.

I didn't expect Paul to think much of the cardigan, but after the barkeep brought over the two beers, a plate of cheddar cheese, and a small glass of Wild Turkey (from the top shelf) for me, I came back to it. At least appreciate the particulars of the deal: the number of units, price per, and the difficulty in securing the right zipper. How many textile mills were still operating in Kensington? I asked him, rhetorically. His eyes blinked but he didn't answer. Well, first of all, more than you think. I listed the names of a dozen mills and manufacturers just in a few square blocks, each one hanging on, somehow. Paul asked me what they make. He had his elbows on the table. We'd always said Paul is like me and Alan like Harriett, but Paul is fair like she is and he has her austere emerald eyes. Only Harriett's son would fixate on the sweater. After all this. He said it again, Railroad Enthusiast. Shouldn't the Silk Line have a little style? But this wasn't the Silk Line. This was private label. You have to understand the difference. Bureaucrats picked it out. Party henchmen. Engineers. Didn't he know I'm in charge of everything? That's how the mill runs now. The departments are closed. Forget how Pop-Pop did it: I make all the choices. But what made him want to know? I always said Charlene kept his mind in check, kept him focused. He loses it so easily. She had real goals. She had a perfect vision of the life she wanted.

He barely touched the beer. I explained to him that inside each mill around the neighborhood that might look empty, closed-up, abandoned, some beat up people are assembling something, a machine tool, a ball bearing, a carpet pad, a lampshade, or they were making parts to keep old machines running. An urge came over me to make sure my son would understand the single idea that governed everything: survival.

Paul Silk

My father and I sat at a small table inside the corner taproom. Did the place have a name? We'd come through a side door, "ladies entrance." I faced the bar: varnished wood, perhaps mahogany, long mirror, green lights. Team pictures were taped to the mirror. 1975 Phillies. 1973-74 Flyers, "Stanley Cup Champions." The bar, that is the varnished wood itself, brass fittings, the beer tap, was the nicest thing I'd seen since coming down the steps at the York-Dauphin station. The neighborhood: hadn't most of the old mills shut down? "They feel a noose," he said, and added, "and they're tightening it themselves." So he did notice the worn and gray and limpid air of the place, cloistered, close in, afraid? The voices of the men in the bar registered in the same high compressed key. Do they breathe here? Could they even imagine there is a place called Denver?

As we entered the place, a man at the bar, without looking up (he must have seen us in the mirror), muttered, "Doc's here." The tone was familiar, yet nearly belligerent. Both in equal parts. The bartender said, "What'll you have, Doc?" Doc…my father hadn't even a college degree. But he owned the mill. Was "Doc" a way to put a label on the Jew from Wynnefield dressed in gray slacks and a blazer? The bartender was gruff, but also tender.

I started to tell my father about what had happened that morning outside the newspaper building but for some reason he was still fixated on the sweater he showed me in the office the mill was making for Conrail. Instinctively, I had put it on. Why do I have to put my hands on everything? "Like it's your own skin," you used to say, Charlene. It was lumpy. The zipper caught. The material was cheap. He said it again, as he had once in a letter, "We have to survive." How could I respond? The sweater wasn't merely out of fashion, Charlene, and so I couldn't help it, I pressed him. Wasn't there a designer on staff, a design department like Pop-Pop had?

He got sick of my questions and turned them around. Now I had to answer about my interview at the paper, and what was that about? More confusion, more distortion. Had I invented the scene on Broad Street? The whole business of Rizzo shutting down the press was unfathomable. But it really had happened. "Like the fascism we fought against," my father said, and finally, Charlene, it was just father and son. Is that what was going on? He was talking quieter than usual, as if he didn't want the people in the bar to hear us talking about, what? Serious things? But here he was "Doc." The dark paneling made the place look even more out of time, insular. The sun outside was bright, but you couldn't know it here. Then, again. "The only thing that matters here in Kensington is survival."

"You're going back there for the interview?" he jabbed.

I nodded. I couldn't tell him I hated to be a reporter. But maybe he would understand. Only this is the life he chose. No: the life he fell into. Aside from the war, he's come here to his neighborhood every day for almost forty years. He wasn't quite comfortable with me coming in (one entered Kensington as if it was another world). He tossed back the glass of Wild Turkey and quickly finished the beer. He left the cheese sandwiches for me. It's very possible he's spent more time here, in this crusty taproom, than any other public place in the city.

When it seemed like I'd had enough, he put four dollars on the table. He put his hands in his pockets as we started to walk out. Then the voice from the bar with the familiar belligerence: "Hey, Doc, how come you don't ever hire white?"

8.

Paul Issues an Invitation

Paul Silk

I have been known to erupt with an idea, a notion, an urge. Is this the Russian or the German in me? The eruption may be overwhelming of reason, especially as I begin to shape the idea or announce it to someone else (I strain to hear you laughing wherever you are—this is how I came to propose so early in our courtship). As you know the eruption will produce one of two kinds of mind: the clear mind and the cloudy mind (is one of *these* the Russian or the German in me? Sometimes it is hard to tell. Well, it may depend, and still you must be laughing, my dear Charlene). My mind sharpened on the day I proposed. The love, it was clear, could overcome the obvious challenges. Other eruptions become muddled from the first, an expression of the absurd, irrational, rash. They lead to the opposite of intent, or even desire. I run toward instead of away from the fire. Such was the case on Friday March 26, 1976.

Elsa Franklin Smith

Sometimes the phone would ring around ten in the morning when it was most quiet here. The coffee and cream I had made hours before would be cold and I'd toss in a couple of ice cubes and a touch of sugar and I'd have iced coffee until lunch. Long time ago I learned to sip my coffee slow. Charlene would call me then, when she was getting ready to go to work. She'd say, "Granny, I just wanted to hear your voice." Usually a Friday, like today. I had a terrible premonition that it was the police calling when the phone rang this morning, March 26, about five after ten. I hadn't heard Monte come in and I didn't know if he was in his room. He keeps that door shut. There was silence on the other end of the line for a while and I said, "Hello, hello, who's there?" Then I heard Paul's voice clear as a bell. I don't want to admit it but just that night I had dreamed that Paul was the one who died, not Charlene. And so hearing his voice through the telephone shocked me, for only a second, but long enough. What do they say, cat's got my tongue.

"Granny? Granny? You there?"

He said something like that. Hmm. I try to stay sharp but on occasion I can't catch right up. He said he just wanted to let me know he hadn't forgotten about me. The boy is sweet and I have missed him. I gather he wanted something, in any case. Tell me how you are, I said. He started telling me about the newspaper and union men blocking them from putting out the paper. They shoved him to the ground! Eventually, he got his interview and an offer for a job. As he was describing it to me he paused a while, as if distracted, and then I recognized a different tone I hadn't heard in a while. Miss Elsa, they used to say, "she knows how to listen" or "she hears what you can't hear, just watch her, you'll see." So I could tell something was coming. His voice expanded out like a song on the record player that surprises you because suddenly it starts playing. Something he'd thought of excited him. He stopped himself from telling me about the newspaper and the blockade and the interview. All of a sudden he was going on about a pizzeria, the one at the corner of 61st and Lansdowne. He didn't know the name of it. I told him I believed it was called Olivetti's. "Can you make it there tonight?"

I wasn't sure. I don't usually like pizza. I told him this and recognizing his tone of voice, I said, "Slow down a minute, Paul." I had to get it straight. "Tell me what you have in mind." He asked if Anita and Charles had plans that evening. "Plans? No, they don't have plans." He may have noticed how my voice had gone quiet.

He said, like a spoon stirring, "OK, they do now." He gave me the time, six-thirty, and reminded me of the corner. "It's actually very good, better than good, you'll see."

I let him be quiet for a minute and then I asked, "Do you want us to invite Monte and Jeanette, too?"

He seemed a little startled by this question. Maybe he hadn't thought of it. And then I thought to myself even if I wasn't sure it was exactly true, "Paul doesn't always know what he wants."

He said, "Sure, if they want to come."

I said, "You're sure?"

He said, "Granny, whoever wants to come, should. It's Friday night pizza." He said this last part as if it signified something in particular.

"OK," I replied. Then he repeated how good the pizza was and he said he was going to try to reach his mother at school so that she wouldn't make other plans. That's how I understood that what he was trying to do was keep his two families together.

Harriett Silk

Quite a few of the Wynnefield Jews had their beloved Overbrook pizza places, where they would go on a Friday night. Falconelli's I think was the usual favorite. There were others, too, and each family, it seemed, had their reasons why their place was better than the others. It might have been the thin crust, the sweet sauce, or just the right amount of cheese or oregano. Each family had a high degree of loyalty, even ownership, over this custom, as if it had been imported from the Old World. Who knows? Perhaps we might trace it to ancient Rome. Another way to think about it: If it wasn't for the Jews the Italians would never have prospered. But for some reason, we never developed this Friday night pizza habit, even though we were often invited to go with other families. Some of these families keep up this tradition, even after their children move out and they move, as we did, to Bala, or as far as Penn Valley. Something compels them back in. I think it is to assuage their guilt at moving out. Sam might have liked it if we had a regular Friday night pizza place, but he never mentioned anything about it.

So I was somewhat surprised when my son called me at school and it was to arrange to go for pizza on Friday. This was one of those ideas of his, like marrying a black girl. I'm still inclined to give him what he wants, even though Charlene had been dead for over a year and he'd been home nearly a month. Which place? Naturally, I wanted to know so that I could call Sam and make the arrangements. Paul wasn't sure of the name. He thought perhaps Oliveri's. 61st and Lansdowne? How had he heard of it? It wasn't far from the high school. Was it one of those places where the kids hang out? He'd gone there one day and he found the owner to be decent and the pizza "surprisingly good." I had my doubts, but I was rushed. The bell was about to ring. "It seemed like he could really use the business." I acquiesced. Paul has been gone for a while. Everything looks new to him. He sees what we no longer see. At least when I get home, after a week's immersion in Act Four of *Romeo and Juliet*, I won't have to cook dinner.

Charles Johnson

I got me a warm afternoon and it's Friday. I park the truck, easy, right at 61st and Columbia. Good enough so I can keep an eye on it, but not too close, like it's in everyone's way. I come in to change because I'm going over to Mr. G's Starlight and have a taste. The world can do whatever it wants to.

I'm not even sure anyone is in the house. It's quiet. I open some windows in the bedroom, that's how warm it feels. That's when you know the earth is owned by the birds because it sounds like a tropical forest. Is this Brazil? No, man! I closed my eyes for a second…

Granny was sitting there in the window when I came down. I wasn't sneaking. No, I told her straight out what I was doing. She saw I'd gotten changed. The woman knows everything. I had to run back upstairs for my billfold. I come back down, slipped on my jacket, stepped into the vestibule, onto the cracked tile floor you think I'll ever fix? Here comes Granny's voice. She says something like, Be back by quarter past six. Quarter past six? Quarter past six. She tells me we're going to some pizza joint because Paul, my son-in-law, is back in town. Pizza? Yes, dear, she says, in her Granny voice. Right down the block. Not that Olivetti's place? How'd I know? She wants to know how I know. Forget it, I tell her, it's Friday night. I been sliding Butterscotch Krimpets onto shelves all week. The weather's all right. I come back out of the vestibule because I just can't help it. I never have and never will show that woman disrespect. Paul's back? You speak to him? He's OK? He's as good as he could be. Those were her exact words. We're all that way. I told Granny half past six. It doesn't take any time to walk to Olivetti's. Olivetti's, they're gonna make me go in there?

Sam Silk

Olivetti's was the kind of place where you would go for a slice for twenty-five cents. Teenagers hung out there, maybe a few families on Friday night. But it wasn't like Falconelli's, an institution. As Eddie pulled up there right at six-thirty, he asked if I was sure. He suggested he would wait with me until the others showed up. Naturally, everyone else was late. I decided to wait on the corner. The sun had set but the air was comfortable. Trash all over the street. Every one of these guys is just trying to survive and none of them know what's coming. Everyone wants his little piece. You get yours, I get mine. You grow up in a row house, that's enough. But don't give it up. Don't lose it to anybody. That's the mindset. The blacks want more, maybe somebody owes it to them, but who the hell is going to give it up? So we had a war of attrition and Harriett and I had enough. When we moved two miles across the city line we acquired a new freedom. It gave us some power back. Paul thought we were being indifferent or even indolent. But Christ we felt relieved: we had washed our hands of the city.

Olivetti, is it Frank? Frank Olivetti, must be his name. Who lives here anymore, who has the money to keep his place going? Paul picked up on it and wants to give the guy business, charity business. Maybe Paul thinks this is how to save the world. I can't blame him. What will Mr. Olivetti do? He'll try a while wanting to keep his restaurant going. The place was probably started by his grandfather in 1948 with a recipe brought over in 1912. The story is always the same. Fill a need, make some money then decide, at the right time, to move or sell. Conserve the wealth and pass it down. If you miss the chance, you can't afford to move or sell? Or you don't want to? Buy lower grade mozzarella for your pizzas. Tell yourself the recipe is still the same. Lie to yourself as long as you can.

Elsa Franklin Smith

We came right down 61st Street to the pizzeria. On the way there Charles tried to tell me the owner was no good, and, of course, I knew what he meant, but I said, anyway, "We'll see." I must have said that ten times between the house and the pizzeria, "we'll see." Charles is the type of son-in-law who will walk with you, and his arm was linked in mine. I'm not slowing down, but it's good to keep steady, especially with the broken, uneven sidewalks and the tree roots that grow however they like getting in the way. The sidewalks are narrow, not like they are on Chestnut Street, so this meant Anita walked behind.

Charles was so much bigger and taller than Sam Silk. This is the kind of thing, like we used to say when we'd see Wilt Chamberlain around the neighborhood, "he's so much taller than he looks on television." Most of us had pretty small screens. Charles wasn't nearly as tall as Mr. Chamberlain, but standing there on the corner with the neon red and green from the window sign flashing, Sam appeared diminished, a small man. And Sam tried to cover a forlorn and confused expression with his sheepish smile. He really was confused. He didn't seem to be aware that we had been invited to the dinner at the pizzeria. Standing there alone next to the tall stacks of milk crates because Paul and Harriett hadn't yet arrived, he tried to make some sense of the situation. Charles didn't seem to notice Sam's state and so when Sam came near, kissed me softly on the cheek, and said, "Such a lovely surprise to see you, Elsa," I said to him, "Sam Silk, we're all going to have some pizza for Paul, for this new job at the paper." And he said, "Yes we will." From that minute, Sam became festive and while Charles kept up the air of reserve he sometimes gets around white folk, even family, and Anita stared into space, Sam and I kidded about Paul's "brilliant ideas."

We had just decided to go in and get a table when Harriett and Paul pulled up in the car. Harriett had on a very fashionable blouse with ruffled sleeves and a long skirt under her coat. Sam was lucky for such an intelligent and vibrant woman. Jewish women like Harriett are raised to be equal to their brothers. Charlene admired Harriett's mother, Simone, for this reason. Well, even if her husband wasn't, Harriett seemed quite prepared to see us outside that pizzeria at 61st Street and Lansdowne Avenue.

Michael Olivetti

When that kid with the bushy hair and the short neck came in I could tell right away he was in some kind of trouble. He was white as a ghost. Looks like he could probably use a priest, I said to myself, and I told Ann-Marie to see what he needed. For a minute I started to think he was a fighter from the gym on Lancaster Avenue. He was stocky and unshaved, and sweating. As soon as I heard him talk I realized I was wrong; you can usually tell who someone is from what they say and how they talk. He was probably a Jew or a teacher. Maybe he just got jumped by a kid from the neighborhood. He came out of the bathroom and I could tell without seeing him any more than from the corner of my eye that he was mulling something. I already decided to have Ann-Marie bring him out a slice before he even said a word. My brother, may he rest in peace, would have said, "Sorry, buddy, come back when you get a little change in your pocket." His eyes cut through everything like that, my brother. I never believed for a second the guy would come back. Ann-Marie said to me, "Uncle Mike, I bet he will." She has an open heart like my mother. "He liked your pizza, Uncle Mike. He'll come back."

He better have liked the pizza. When my brother was killed, I didn't change anything about the pizza recipe, but I decided to stop cheaping out on the ingredients. The tomatoes we were using were no good and the mushrooms came from a can. I took a little of the money he left and started to fix the place up. For now, I've left the sign our father installed in 1961, and I still change the fluorescent bulbs inside any time one goes out. I hate the blinking—makes it look like we're dirty and poor. White, with Olivetti's in blue script, and on both sides of the corner, 61st and Lansdowne. The only problem is I lost the "e" on the Lansdowne side and I don't know how to get it replaced. I painted the apartments upstairs and put in new tile in the bathrooms. Nobody wants a bathroom with pink tile in it anymore. Inside the shop, I got started on the walls. With the Bicentennial coming up I made the theme about the brotherhood of Italy and America. I have Independence Hall and the Liberty Bell, because we ought to be more proud of our city and we better not forget all the Founding Fathers did for us. They gave my people freedom, whether they knew it or not. Next to that, on the other part of the wall, I had the kid who painted everything, he's in the art program at West Catholic High School, I had him paint the white cliffs of Lecce and the turquoise water of the Adriatic Sea. And I had him paint the San Giovanni Battista church where the Olivettis used to be baptized, and a traditional *trullo*, with a cone-shaped roof, which came out beautiful on the wall, and I only had an old black and white picture to show the kid. Everyone thinks if you're Italian in Philly that you came from Catania or somewhere else in eastern Sicily, or Naples. No one thinks Puglia, the heel of the boot. The stiletto heel, my friend. That's why the classic Olivetti pizza comes with anchovy, I don't want anyone to forget the Italian families who came to Overbrook. Maybe they came to South Philly first, but the most successful ones, the ones who learned how to stop suffering, came up here. 1925, 1928 or so. And why should we be chased out? My brother Sandro was about to give up on this place when he was killed. Does that mean I'm defying his memory? He always said he never understood me, but I know that isn't true. After the kid was done painting the San Giovanni church, I had him add Saint Rose of Lima, the parish church right here on Lansdowne Avenue. Then I had a portrait of Frank Rizzo framed and I hung it above the pizza oven, next to John Kennedy and the Pope.

Harriett Silk

I let Paul and his in-laws and Elsa and Sam go in before me and sit down. I followed, but not too closely, as I needed some distance. What sort of place was Olivetti's? A glorified hole-in-the-wall, with a girl at the counter, above her a black menu board with removable white letters. Slice .25¢, slice with pepperoni .30¢, Olivetti's classic $2.95, chicken cutlet sandwich with provolone cheese and long hots $1.75, meatball sandwich $1.50, veal filet with spaghetti $3.25. Will there be table service? The girl at the counter smiled at me. A tenth grader, I imagine, fifteen or sixteen years old. Behind her, a slender, balding man works the pizza oven. It doesn't occur to me until I see it: the portrait of Frank Rizzo. Why do they love him? Because he tells them what they want to hear. Over on the far wall, where booths are, an elaborate mural of an Italian church and next to it, the imagined waters of the Mediterranean, rather mawkish. And there, right above our table, the Italian and American flags, poles crossed, as if it was still 1921.

They made room for me at the end of the booth, across from Elsa. Of all these people, she is the one I wanted to see most. I told Anita and Charles that I wished I had more Jeanettes and Montes in class, what a joy it always was. Charles appeared to be aging. Has he stopped shaving? His beard is going gray. Sam was laughing altogether too loudly. What everyone wanted to hear about was Paul's interview at the paper (which he had told me about in the car on the way over). But as he started to speak, the pizza man came over. Apparently, he'd recognized Paul, his new loyal customer.

He tried to mask his astonishment over our interracial group. If there is one thing Paul's marriage to Charlene (and, to be frank, my long career teaching at Overbrook High School) has taught me, it's to notice the slack jaw and the poisoned eyes that try to cover it up. This man's eyes were quite expressive. Mr. Olivetti, or, judging by his age, Mr. Olivetti, Jr., thanked Paul for returning. He said he was sure he would, he knows a good man when he sees one. Paul, in the corner diagonal from me, was clearly pleased by the performance. All of a sudden, he reached into his pocket, requiring some contortions, as we were stuffed into the booth, and wriggled out a dollar, which he handed to our new friend. "For your kindness the other day," he said.

No, he couldn't possibly accept the dollar. The back-and-forth went on a while prompting Charles to say, all right, he'd take the dollar if no one wanted it. Well, the pizza man kept the dollar after all that and as he folded it absent-mindedly, he looked right at Paul then the rest of us and announced, "I would have called the police if I were you. I was pretty worried, my friend, almost called and reported it myself. You can't be too careful."

What had happened? All five of us, even Anita, begged to know. Charles, sitting next to Paul, put his arm around him. I don't think any of us tasted the pizza, when finally it came.

Sam Silk

My son tried to change the subject. He tried to say the incident wasn't anything and when the pizza man turned away and returned to the kitchen, Paul said he was the kind of shopkeeper who exaggerated the problem of crime. Charles turned to Paul and then to me across the table as if I was his ally and would corroborate his story, and, shaking his head, suggested the pizza man was right, and he ought to know. My wife, at the end of the table, was suddenly curious. Charles, trying to be discreet, explained that the pizza man's brother had been murdered at their mother's house on 59th Street. Had his throat slit. Mafia? Yes, of course it was mafia, I whispered, but my son, anxious to turn the conversation, cut me off. He said he was intrigued by the Olivetti's classic pizza with anchovies. He used that word, intrigued. He looked around the table at each of us, one at a time, to see if anyone else would agree. He was counting on his mother, but the mood had shifted since the pizza man had come over. Olivetti's no longer seemed so quaint. Charles laughed. He'd eaten enough anchovies in 1943 for a lifetime. Anita admitted the idea didn't appeal all that much to her. But she suggested that since the dinner was in honor of Paul he should have whatever he wanted. I was starting to feel a little hungry. I wanted to order. The anchovy pie was out of the question, but I wasn't sorry the conversation had turned from whatever had happened to Paul. I just didn't want to talk about crime with Charles and Anita. For Christ's sake, and in this Italian joint, too. It made me nervous. Now a girl came over to take the order. I looked right at Charles and we agreed without even a sound trespassing between us, a plain, a pepperoni, and an onion, and if that was too much, we'd have lunch for tomorrow.

Paul Silk

Change the subject, change the subject! "There you go, baby, obfuscating," you used to say, and this time I had to. I had to keep Monte out of it. But carefully now, I looked around the table. Your mama, Charlene, held her gaze on me, for once. Did she know? How could I burden her more? Your daddy looked over at my father, but what for? And Sam kept expecting my mother to say something, but she didn't. She can't stand to overreact. And Granny, she took my hand in hers. It was warm just like yours. I didn't want them to care. I didn't want anyone to care. The rumors in the newsroom: maybe the tide is turning on Rizzo, his grip loosening. Not here, I could hear my mother say. Not in a place like this. Would Rizzo pay for locking down the paper? Did he have anything to lose? He'd won reelection last year with fifty-five percent.

"Well?" my mother asked.

"Do you want to hear what they're saying at the paper?" I asked.

Granny squeezed tighter. "You don't have to hide it from us," she said.

"Paul, man. It's none of our business," your daddy said.

"Christ, Paul, tell us about Frank Rizzo later," my father said. "We can handle it."

"It's nothing," I said. "The recall campaign is for real. I heard it from ten different reporters. Now he's raised water and sewer rates. You saw that: the largest increase in history. He's going to send a huge tax hike to Council."

"You can't recall him for that," my mother said.

"Paul," said Granny, and I could swear it was you.

"And shut Philadelphia General for good."

"Close that hospital?" This was your daddy. "Where will the poor folk go?"

"Paul," said your mama. She started to say something more, but just then the waitress brought over our salads, each one in a little wooden bowl. She set down the oil and vinegar in the center of the table.

"There's not a single place in Denver," I offered, "where you can get oil and vinegar in these little bottles, they don't know anything about it there."

"I should think not," said my mother. But then, "Well?"

"Well what?"

"What happened to you, Sonny?" asked Granny.

"We're celebrating tonight. I'm back in the newsroom." But I couldn't avoid Granny's side-glance, which you must have learned from her, even as I picked among the red onion, cherry tomatoes, the brine of oil and vinegar. You won't be with me in the newsroom.

It isn't a celebration at all.

Granny reached over again, across your daddy, and with her hand on mine, said, "Paul wanted those anchovies!"

I tried to say the oil and vinegar was good enough, the anchovies too salty, but blushing now, words leaping around, Charlene. I lost control of them and they scattered away: "I'm an idiot for hiding the truth. Forgive me."

"Forgive you? For what?" said my mother.

"I had an altercation with Monte."

"What sort of altercation?" She couldn't help herself. "What sort?" She looked over at your mama and then at my father, as if it could have been his fault.

Your daddy put down his fork, but all he said was, "that's crazy," as if I was talking about someone else's son. Your mama swallowed and apologized. I didn't even hear what she said.

"No, Anita, don't apologize," my mother said.

I needed to stand, but instead I spoke a little slower and quieter, downplaying the danger and also the look on Monte's face. They couldn't know that he had scared me. "I don't know how to make sense of it," I said instead. He's bottled up with resentment, fear of his own self, and haunted by the war. I couldn't say that either, or mention you. You took care of your own life, Charlene, and not his.

"I can't lock him in the house," your daddy said, with defensive pride he didn't need. But he couldn't help it. Who could help it?

"The Monte I know has poise, he has a mind. I've taught almost forty years."

"But the war broke him, Harriett," said Granny, "and I can't seem to recall how it happened. But, we can't lose sight of the kind of boy he was."

"That would be a crime, Elsa," said my mother.

"Imagine he'd do that to Paul, Harriett," replied Granny, "as if he's become someone else."

"My son," was all your mama could manage.

Then the pizza came. Your daddy's hand overwhelmed the limp slice of pizza, like a bear's paw clenching a fish. But tears spun in his eyes.

"The whole thing was just as much my doing as his," I said.

"No, no," said your daddy. "Don't take it away from him."

"The old Monte is still there, he must be," said my mother. Did she mean it? I've never heard her speak of another student the way she does Monte.

But Monte, your brother. It's his own legendary intellect he's turned on, using it for and against himself, twisting it as a clever criminal would. The leftist cell you followed all the way to the government laboratory, Charlene, you remember? You listened to them, but you couldn't understand, because they wouldn't accept culpability, even if they blew up the laboratory. They had hardened themselves, as if they didn't have hearts. What happened to Monte's heart? When you were kids and Jeanette a baby, you told me, he would sit on your lap on that brown rug with the red circle. He always wanted to sit in that circle and that meant you had to move the heavy glass table. "You can move it, Charlene, you can move it," he would say. He made you do it so that he could sit in the red circle, but on your lap. You said his feet dug into the plush of the rug, his feet got lost in the rug.

My father finished his soda, folded one arm over the other. "The pizza isn't bad," he said, "Paul, you were right. Never doubt Paul." But then he turned to your daddy. I don't think he was expecting it, he doesn't know what to do with Monte. Politely, my father asked your daddy, "What do you think? If he has it in him, I will give him a way, it's the least I could do. He can come work with me personally at the mill. I will see to it that he has a chance. What do you think?"

Your daddy, Charlene, I have seen it before. He was grateful, but filled with worry. Only obstacles seemed to come out his mouth. "No black cat is gonna be safe in Kensington! Not that Monte couldn't handle it, but history is history. Maybe you know better, Sam."

Even in Kensington things are changing, "in the Bicentennial year it is finally changing," my father replied. He turned to your mama for some reason then and she nodded silently.

"This is Paul's night, don't let us forget," said your daddy.

"And we have Paul to thank for helping his brother," said Granny. Her wish was coming true.

My mother hated the idea of Monte working in the mill. She glared at my father. But he only said, "There's work, that's all."

Sam Silk

When I noticed the tears building up in Charles' eyes, not out of sadness but out of shame, and probably frustration, and likely exhaustion, I decided I had to do something. These people are family and, frankly, we owe it to Charlene. I don't know exactly what I'm going to do, or if the risk is greater for me or for Monte, but there's no use staying on the sidelines. It's a matter of the kid's survival. Once we finally made it through the meal, I took Charles aside and we got in his Tasty Kake delivery van. I didn't want to talk to Paul about this, or Harriett. I told Charles I had no guarantees. Was it even clear a job would straighten him out? It seemed to me his troubles ran deeper. The kid is intelligent, maybe he's creative, and he has some skills. An army medic is like a handyman. He keeps bodies running.

That's good enough for me. Is he crazy? I've heard of Vietnam vets who can't stop killing. Kensington fights everything. Silk Industries has survived for seventy years, goddammit. But I told Charles it's up to Monte. Charles should ask him and if Monte says yes tell him that's good enough for me.

Charles Johnson

Sam Silk is all right, I mean as far as people in this world go, there are worse. He comes over by the jukebox they got at Olivetti's and says he wants to talk. Now? Shit. Yes, now. My back was killing me from that booth and us squeezed in. I wanted to lay myself out. Saturday used to be an off day, but no more. And this cat wants to talk. He wants to talk Monte, but I say fine, Sam, you ever been to Mr. G's? Anita took Granny home and we got in the truck, pulled up in front of the joint, and went in. This is an equal opportunity city. There used to be a white guy sat down the end of the bar, squirrel of a man, red nose, beady little eyes. He was all right, didn't bother no one. One time tried to break up a fight, lost his own false teeth and hit his head on the bathroom sink. Mr. G doesn't like fighting and he paid for the oldtimer's medical bills. Said it was his responsibility.

We went in and I introduced Sam around and said that we had some shit to deal with. It's dark in Mr. G's, but I could tell he wasn't fazed by it. And why should he? We all live here on the same sweet earth, us and all the birds. We took a table under the neon sign. I made it like I was the one wanted to talk to him, because now I did, and so I got started and asked him why he wanted to step in? Nobody needs a white savior. What can you do for him that I can't? He didn't try to answer. He just said he could give Monte a job, couldn't guarantee nothing more. If Monte says yes he should be ready Monday morning early. Sam was afraid of getting too far in, so he kept the whole thing at a distance. My thing is when Monte's in your mill there won't be any distance. So think it over? But Sam had made his mind up. He looked worn down, like a lead pencil and there's no knife or sharpener around.

I took him home and he told me to call him as soon as I talk to Monte. Sooner the better, he said. Man lives in the woods.

I had on some white bread junk on the TV about a dog that's saved five kids from drowning when Monte slid in the door. He barely needs to open it to fit in. Surprised myself what came out of my mouth. I sit in that truck for hours every afternoon crying because I don't want to lose you. Something like that came right out. So listen, don't fuck it up. Go to work at Sam Silk's shop on Monday, and keep your head down. See if it's all right. It won't reverse time, now I was crying, it won't bring nothing back. He stood there then he sat down. He was graceful when he was seventeen, could glide across the room. He still gets around like that. Don't know where he learned it, who he stole it from.

Paul? That's what he said, just like that staring at the TV. Paul? No, Paul has nothing to do with it. Then he glassed over. More like he pulls the shades down into the darkness. He sat up real straight, his face empty of expression, and though I was crying harder now I heard him say, Fine. He sat there, still like that, for ten, fifteen minutes, didn't say another word. I dialed Sam and gave him the news.

9.

What's the Story
with Silk Industries?

Sam Silk

Here then are some facts: When my grandfather, Shmuel, who I am named for, the man who started Silk Industries, decided to retire, he gave the company, in even shares, to his sons, Abe and Harry. Shortly after, Harry enlisted in the army and was sent to France to fight in the Great War, World War One. Harry escaped the war with only an injured shoulder from which the military surgeons had removed some shrapnel. But Harry, who up until that point had always seemed like he would become the rich and successful brother, lost his ambition during the war. At the same time he'd become enamored of the simple life of the old world. After his injury he'd found a small village in the Southern Alps where he was given fresh cheese from sheep and goat milk and fresh bread and coffee that was still abundant despite the war. He returned to Philadelphia a changed man. Harry had lost the taste for profit and couldn't imagine living with the pressure of running Silk Industries. At first, my father, Abe, was disappointed. He'd dreamed of spending his life working with his witty younger brother Harry. He tried all kinds of ways to convince him; he proposed that Harry would be in charge of design and Abe sales and operations. At the time we produced yarns for use in carpets and clothing items, like undergarments and sweaters, as well as a series of "fancies" for specialty embroidery—a line for which my father was justifiably proud. This set us apart from the competition. In those days there were dozens of mills in the textile sector, in Kensington and Manayunk, usually owned by the sons or grandsons of an original immigrant. Those original immigrants were typically German. The rare Jews like us—and Russian Jews, too, I might add—had bought up someone's operation at fire sale. Competition was rough.

Each little company prided itself on doing one or two things well. There were loomers, weavers, carpet men, embroiderers, and men who did all these things in silk, to make hosiery and the like. Some produced fabric, upholstery, drapes, cushions, and some cut and others dyed. The dye houses would take your yarn and color it to specifications. My father would go over to the dye house on Torresdale Avenue and look through the color charts and if the dye didn't match he'd go back, in person, bring over a pair of cigars, one for him and one for the floor manager, or the foreman, or even the owner, a businessman like he was, and smoke the cigars until they got it right. In those days, and even until I was a boy of ten or eleven, the dye houses would dry the yarns by driving them in the open air around the neighborhood, up and down the cobbled streets in a horse-led truck. Almost everyone used the dye houses not only for coloring the yarn that would be used for carpets or drapes or felt or underwear, but for cutting, finishing, warehousing, and even distribution. A few mills—no more than a dozen of them, if I had to guess—did all of this in-house, but those typically specialized in one thing, like hats, and they wanted control of the manufacturing process. The best example of this, the one everybody knows, is Stetson, which closed only a few years ago, 1971. The thing is, if you were a mill owner, you might feel constrained producing only one line or one piece of raw material. So you would add something and discover you could move your workers around, keep the old, loyal ones by giving them a new job that was easier on the feet and on the back. And that was one reason for adding a division or bringing some function in-house. After Harry quit, my father built up an entire division just for design and some smaller firms would come to him because he employed graphic artists and even fashion designers. This is the way things worked in Kensington. Each owner made deals with five or six others who produced something he needed.

My father relished the dealing, but he also liked to figure things out, like a puzzle. But he thought he could do this better with Harry, and he felt this way so strongly that even if they didn't split the work evenly they would still split the profits fifty-fifty. Harry considered the offer and for a while the two brothers tested the arrangement. But soon Harry realized he couldn't hack it. Competition among woolen mills was high as ever and some of Harry and Abe's competitors had figured out how to cut costs by moving some or all of their operation to a place like Tennessee or Georgia, where labor was cheap. In order to find a way out, Harry accused Abe of reneging on the fifty-fifty split. Harry married Fanny then and withdrew my parents' invitation to the wedding. Seeing this, my father, a fair and giving man, offered to buy out Harry's share of the company plus a percentage of future proceeds (business boomed in the 1920s). With this cash, Harry bought a house on Osage Avenue, only two blocks from ours, and opened his hardware store on 60th Street. This was all he needed in the world.

For years, my father and his brother existed this way, in peace and equanimity. Aunt Fanny couldn't have kids, but she lavished attention on my sister, Shelly, and me. But slowly we moved up and Harry and Fanny stayed the same. Prohibited from joining Philmont (no Russian Jews or tradesmen allowed), my parents helped found the Western Club. They didn't ask Harry and Fanny to join.

Harry will always tell you he moved into the Lebanon Arms to keep Betty company in old age, as if this was some great sacrifice. But the truth was that when Fanny died, two years after Abe, Harry had no money left. For years he'd kept the hardware store going on their savings; the store hadn't turned a profit since 1959. And we, not wanting to see the man destitute, and, if you're inclined analyze it, secretly guilty for his poverty (and decades of unfortunate envy), found him the apartment that just happened to be on my mother's floor, and put down the deposit. And every month since then my mother has paid his rent.

Alan Silk

Naturally, I assured my mother I would do whatever I could for Paul. "Get him a haircut, his hair's gotten so bushy." I'm not going to get him a haircut. A thirty-one-year-old man. But I will take him for a proper lunch. And so I told him to meet me at the Sansom Street Oyster House at twelve-thirty and hope you arrive hungry.

I think I chose well. He couldn't take his eyes off the hands of the waiter shucking the oysters and opening the clams. This was something new. And he kept saying, "Wow, this is really good." I sat back, with my tie tucked into my shirt to protect it from splattering juices, and watched him, a little like a child, eating and making a mess, and it brought me right back to the kitchen on 53rd Street. Something about the position of the table and our hands and me, the older brother, looking down on him and waiting for him to finish eating. Always so slow.

"How long has dad had a driver?" he asked, all of a sudden. "Who is this guy picks him up every morning like he's some kind of don?"

"You mean Eddie?"

"And sometimes there's another guy, shorter, fatter."

"Dad's always trying to find these guys some work."

He gazed again, intently. Fidgeted with the salt. His fingers stubby, as if somehow roots squirreling around under the earth. "A charity? The mill is a charity?"

"He's always run the place that way."

"Do you know about the business? I mean sales, production—"

"He guards the balance sheets like a hawk."

"I thought you might be an exception."

"I never ask."

"Let's say you did. Would you ever maybe wonder if the mill was some kind of front? How many sweaters could Silk Industries make?"

"Remember we used to have to wear the sweaters."

"Designed by Pop-Pop."

"You hated the itch."

"You hated it, too!"

"I hated them because they looked old-fashioned, the same design

THE YEAR OF THE RETURN

as 1945. I never understood who bought them," I said.

"Exactly. Who buys them now, Alan? Who besides Conrail?"

"For one, the teacher's union. They embroider 'Federation of Teachers' on them."

A little oyster meat was hanging from his beard. I'd been staring at it for ten minutes. Finally, I brushed it off. He thanked me. He wasn't embarrassed. Why does he need to know all this annoying stuff? Better to be in Denver. He started fidgeting again. The tiffany lamp reflected in his eyeglasses. When he looked up, finally, his eyes glowed red.

Albert Birnbaum

"He has terrific discretion" isn't the highest compliment a lawyer can receive, but it is gratifying nonetheless to be thought of in this way. It indicates that I, as an attorney, am very likely to treat a client's private affairs, his business dealings, his tax returns, and his investments with extreme, even vigilant care. An attorney with a practice like mine values individuals over corporations and political concerns over constitutional ones. This doesn't mean he operates without an ideological or moral framework. For instance, over many years I repelled the entreaties of Frank Rizzo, who believes that the only kind of good lawyer is a Jewish lawyer.

Discretion thus has a double edge. An attorney with discretion is expert at keeping things hidden and deciding when they ought not be hidden any more. My brother-in-law, Samuel Silk, has been my client almost since the moment I began to practice the law, in 1947. Sam is the husband of my older sister, Harriett. He won a Bronze Star for bravery during the Second World War. After the war, he became the vice president of Silk Industries, the company owned by his father, Abraham. In 1961, Sam became the president. At that time, we devised and executed a generous buy-out of Sam's sister Sherry's portion of the company, effectively thirty-three percent. (Sherry, an anthropologist, had moved to Montreal.) When Abe died in 1966, his wife, Sam and Sherry's mother, Betty, retained her one-third share of Silk Industries. A lesson for anyone who doesn't believe in the American dream, or thinks it mere myth: Betty's father, Moses Gordon, from the village of Vitebsk, was the driver for Shmuel Silk, Abraham's father, and the man who established Silk Industries. Another lesson, if you are paying attention: many people, and various families, have depended upon and profited from the wealth generated by Silk Industries. As a person entrusted with the documents, reports, tax filings, and legal obligations of the company, it is up to my discretion when, and toward what purpose, to reveal certain kinds of information.

It is this use of discretion that I now must weigh. Some of those who know Sam Silk, my client and brother-in-law, may be aware of an attachment to certain kinds of nouns that are also states of being, such as survival, legacy, and privacy, and, not to forget, Philadelphia. My sister Harriett, I am sure, was drawn to Sam's romantic nature when she herself was a young and idealistic graduate of Cornell University. But Harriett's idealism, as time has proven, has been bolstered by rigor. On many occasions, she has been named the Overbrook High School teacher of the year. The issue may not be Sam's attachment to any one of these nouns that are also states of being (though some are more dangerous than others); nor is the attachment evenly distributed. On November 2, 1971, Sam called me in my office. Election Day is a busy day for many attorneys in Philadelphia, but Sam got through. He wanted to tell me that for the first time in his adult life he wasn't voting in the Philadelphia mayoral election, because he and Harriett had moved their residence to Montgomery County. He was gloating. "I've washed my hands of the city," he proclaimed.

I might have known that the attachments can be complicated, none more so than the attachment to privacy. Silk Industries is a privately held, family-operated business. Who, then, in the family, has a right to the information concerning the firm? Harriett? Well, she has seen the tax returns, which she reads as carefully as she reads *Beowulf.* But the tax returns have a way of masking certain truths. The eldest son of Harriett and Sam, my nephew Alan, the insurance executive? His brother, Paul, the journalist who just returned to Philadelphia after the tragic loss of his beautiful wife, Charlene?

THE YEAR OF THE RETURN

Sam's mother, Betty? All of these people have some legal, and possibly statutory, right to information about the company. The question in front of me is whether or not, or to what extent, might I use my discretion in releasing certain points of information? The president of the company put up a fence along the wooded rear border of his residence, but should that fence extend, as a metaphor, around the dollar value of annual sales? Soon enough that number may be too small to adequately hide.

Monte Johnson

Employment Application

Name: Monte I. Johnson

Address: 6147 West Columbia Avenue, Philadelphia, Penna. 19151

Competencies (please list top five in ranked order):

1. Sobriety
2. Camouflage
3. Tracheotomy
4. Diagnosing syphilis
5. ~~Sabotage~~ Search and rescue

Office Skills (please list top five in ranked order):

1. Penmanship
2. Loading staple gun
3. Laying traps
4. Selective hearing
5. Foot dragging

Greatest obstacle overcome:

Reviving a dead man (elephant grass, Mekong Delta, May 8, 1970)

Greatest obstacle not overcome:

Banality (*injustice close second)

Why did you leave your last position?

Radio out! Radio out! Let me set the scene (cue: sweat). Choppers. A daisy chain dangling right over there in the water. You learn to see them on the second day. In the reeds. You know how it is, you show up one day in the reeds stomping along. In the reeds. 1971, we'd already been to Cambodia (only support, mind you). So tired of killing, only wanted to kill, when that's all is left. It's the easiest thing. The whole unit behind or in or under the reeds, all mixed up bloods and whites. Arkansas already gone home. (The unit slipped beyond the reeds, or I did.) Medic! On the radio. Shh, now. I, Monte Johnson, of unsound mind and tight-ass body, was at the river and then I was being shown something, a human person inside a hut with a thatched roof. It was a person, a mama, like a leaf that could blow away. Help? I can't make this shit up (on fake-as-shit job application you're allowed to swear). You help? I help. I save Mrs. Tuan. The mama of Tuan. Tuan. Silence, birds, frogs, leaves, smoke, feet stopped sinking in the mud (metaphor), no, I was already out.

Tuan, he say, you stay. Shh.
Me Monte, I say. Where am I?
An Thanh, he say. No place.

The leaves are singing, you, Monte, shh, let the leaves sing. Listen. Boot camp: "It can get very dark in Vietnam at night." Stay here, you work, you doctor. You stay. You sleep next to well. I find you next to well. Every night I find you next to well.

HQ: Medic Monte Irvin Johnson. Status: Slipped Away.

HQ: Medic Monte Irvin Johnson discovered captive in village of An Thanh.

HQ: Rescue sent at 07:00. Village of An Thanh relieved of inhabitants, etc. etc.

Sir, please answer more succinctly. (War lost.)

Describe a time you had to make a difficult decision:

014:00 Zulu, 17 December 1970, 25th Infantry, 2nd Brigade, Plain of Reeds near Cambodian border. During ambush retreat, Medic M.I. Johnson nearly trips over object in the burned grass, making moaning sounds, crying. The object is a man, approximately nineteen years old, staked to the ground, skinned from neck to privates, maggots under arms, in crotch, in intestines, severe blood loss from laceration and flesh ingestion by wild animal. Medical condition: terminal. Soldier makes known wish to die. Medic Johnson administers morphine at high dose, but soldier can't stop crying. Attempting to evacuate soldier will kill him. Soldier begs to die. Medic Johnson waits twenty minutes. Makes second diagnosis. Soldier reaffirms desire to die. Medic Johnson calls into HQ for direction, is instructed to make up his own mind. Medic Johnson covers his mouth and nose to withstand stench of the dying man, asks soldier again if he wishes to die, attains affirmative, eliminates soldier's pain. Thereafter Medic Johnson is known to himself as Dr. Death.

Erectile capacity (how hard is your dick right now—4. extremely, 3. rod-like, 2. ready-for-anything, 1. shriveling, 0. soft-as-shit): 0

Sam Silk

1969, the year Paul and Charlene decided to move away, business began to turn, hard and fast. Until then, Silk Industries had survived by eating up other companies' product lines. I was aggressive about this, anticipating when a firm's margin was heading into the red and offering quick cash. Most of these guys, even the younger ones, either the grandson or great-grandson of the founder, or with a degree in textile engineering, got tired of fighting over crumbs. The ambitious ones were Indian. They came here to learn the trade, and some even stayed, started up new firms making synthetics. But eventually they went home. I never understood why they didn't bring their own dye techniques here to America. But they went back to India or even on to Mexico or China, where they could get paid for their expertise. Textiles had been leaving the city since the 1920s. Now the exodus was merely accelerating with synthetics in carpets, drapery, clothing, you name it. We just couldn't keep up.

My father died in 1966 and even then we were still growing. I kept bringing the reports over to the house, but he'd lost interest. He only wanted to talk about the kids. If I ever wanted his advice about a customer or an employee, he would shrug, as if he'd already gone on to the next world. He still smoked a cigar, my father, all the way to the end.

So he missed the turn. Naturally, I missed the chance to sell. Now, Silk Industries is worth almost nothing. Some young real estate guys are buying old factories in Olde City and turning them into lofts, but I'll be long dead before they get to Kensington. The mill was never the largest, but we were still adding on, even in 1968. But the boiler house is crumbling, the knitting machines and looms ancient, the office outdated. I discovered I could survive by deferring everything, indefinitely.

Then it was barely 1970, 71. The Puerto Ricans were out of control on the other side of the El, in Norris Square. They keep having babies. I can remember when the square itself was decent. You could go over to Front Street, under the El, and get a Breyer's ice cream for a nickel or dime and sit on a bench and stick your face in the sun. In 1970 we were broken into three times. They took the petty cash and some product, then, later, parts, machinery, even wiring. Then some guy got knifed in our courtyard. That's when I hired Eddie and one day it was Louis, too. I didn't question it. This was the way it was going to have to be, dammit. Inventory starting piling up.

Around 1973, Eddie came to me with a proposal. We had recently bought our new house. We needed the cash. He knew what he was doing. Maybe I should have expected it all along. Maybe I should have been wary. Louis was rougher yet easier to please. Eddie doesn't say much. He doesn't need to. Little by little this happened. I let myself be extorted. Did I have a choice? When? They came on like an unstoppable wind that blows harder and harder but you don't notice. There was nothing I could do.

10.

Monday's Coming

Elsa Franklin Smith

If Sam Silk was going to give Monte a chance, I was going to make sure the boy didn't go off somewhere. All weekend I watched him like a hawk. First, I made it a point to talk to him myself, and not rely on Charles or Anita, to prepare him for Monday. I asked him to sit with me and I fed him some chicken salad, which he ate out of the bowl, one tiny piece at a time. His mother was playing the piano, as she does. "Listen to me, Monte Irvin Johnson. My father was never given the chance to work in a factory. Don't you let him down," I said. Did he hear me? Because you know that boy hears only what he wants to. I didn't tell him I knew what he'd done to Paul, as disturbing as it was, but I tried to lead the conversation to where he might offer it himself, but he said in a meager sort of voice, "Granny just got serious."

"I hope the stories I'm hearing about you aren't true," I said, without meaning to. The tone wasn't right, and I thought, "Miss Elsa, now!"

"Any story is true once it's told," he said, I realized it didn't matter what I'd said. This was both comforting and discomforting. Now what's the point of me trying? He leaned over the bowl of chicken salad, which I had just made, and I asked him if it needed more salt. When was the last time we'd sat in the kitchen the two of us? "Drink some iced tea," I said, and poured it out of the yellow pitcher into the glass.

He ate slowly and chewed more than he needed, and what did he mean by that? Monte doesn't do anything without meaning. Nothing by accident. I said it was going to be hard. At first it's going to seem awful and you're going to hate it. I caught his attention this way. You'll have to get up and you'll have to listen and do what you're told.

"Yessir," he said and I know what he meant. He'd taken orders in Vietnam. But that isn't what I meant. His muscles were going to hurt and unless he knew this now he would quit after a day or two.

"You're going to have to put up with pain and then it will give way, like a sore muscle does once it gets used to walking up the hill."

"The wisdom of old black folk," he said.

"Drink your iced tea," I scolded.

No way I would let him go out to the corner. But if I scolded him some more in an hour he would go out there like a magnet for trouble. So I asked him to take me to the Reading Terminal Market. I drew up a list and told him to take the shopping cart down from the hook. "We're going to fill this thing up!" This is how I was going to get him through the weekend: exercising. By Monday he'll be so sore he won't even notice.

Monte Johnson

Needs some salt, Granny.

Add some! Don't need to me to do it.

I don't care.

It needs some, go ahead. Go ahead!

It's all right.

Don't be a fool.

It's all right.

Then don't you eat it.

Why?

You don't like it.

I like it.

But Monte, you said just now, Granny, it needs salt. So put it in.

I like it how it is.

Mind yourself, Sonny. I can't tell what you want. Well?

Nothing.

Monte, this won't do.

Granny, you got some bony fingers.

What, now?

Like a skeleton.

Shush. I am an old skeleton. Nothing funny about it. Spent all those hours scratching your back, these tired hands. Old skeleton scratching your back.

Granny.

Look at your own hands.

(Dr. Death.)

You take after your old Granny.

(They executed Tuan's mama, too. I saved her with their penicillin and they killed her with their slugs. They burned the house. They burned her kitchen.)

You and me, Sonny. Monte! Listen to Granny. Finish up and get on a coat. Let's go catch that trolley.

Charles Johnson

Now we made it our job to get Monte ready. Granny did her damnedest to keep him on a leash. Granny can. The men of this house will always listen to her. All she has to do is slap her hands on her knees and that's it. She fed him and talked his ear off about all kinds of shit and he sat there as if he had no choice in the matter. And all it took was old Sam Silk.

Man, that's the way the white man thinks of it. The white savior. I seen enough of them in the war. But I'll tell you he's all right. I have my doubts about the whole thing, you know the way our two families are all tied up and now the knot's getting tighter instead of looser. You go back a few years and I could dig it, because it was progress. I'm not a stickler for nothing. I'm not gonna get in the way, is what I mean. I was glad to get out the way! Let Charlene run with it. I put on a yarmulke one time. I ate lox and bagels. And matzah. And I never had to explain myself, I'll say that for the Silks. They took the Johnsons as is. But things have turned. You know your kids get married and you go in deep.

Now I didn't go spitting in Paul's eye, but I know I'm going to work starting today at Silk Industries, right? If Monte's going, the way things are, I'm going, somehow. I got to see that he doesn't let Sam down. That he's proper. I thought I'd done that ten years ago and then the cat goes off to Nam. I should have burned his draft card myself. I got to make sure he's proper. Monte sits on the corner. Monte goes into the boarded-up house. Monte says some crazy shit.

And I got my neighbor, Hicks, sits under the clothesline and reads the *Tribune* cover to cover and drinks his ginger beer. He comes from Jamaica. Sometimes I look over there and I get the feeling to go sit with him. It's like a stage set. He rolls a joint and it's all right. I listen to his accent, I watch the laundry dry. It's all right. His wife's big fat bloomers. He puts on some music, some Jamaican music, I don't know where he finds it on the dial. Beats the Phillies. He tries to tell me my son's a homosexual. My first thing is to laugh and then I got to ask, how do you know? For some reason I don't resent Hicks for this. I just don't see it. He's off, but he's not that off. But what if he is? That change anything? He be any more or less Monte? Shit. I can't think of it. I just don't see it. I just don't see it. He's misunderstood. I gave him that name, but he never wanted to play baseball.

11.

First Day of Work

Louis Turner

The phone rings nine o'clock on Sunday night. Do I answer? Who's calling? I got a Hundred Grand Bar in my mouth and I'm trying to chew. Can't talk and chew on that bar at the same time. I let it ring. Rings again. Baby, give it a rest! I put the candy bar down but now I got chocolate all over my hands. Rings again while I got the water running. Someone's trying to get in touch.

It's Eddie. He just starts talking. He has an old man voice on the phone and so at first I'm searching my head for who it is. He's giving me an extra hour in the morning. Eddie? "Yeah it's Eddie." I'm laughing at myself. It's Eddie. Sleep in. Why?

"You got a new helper," he says. So what? "Boss wants us to pick up the new guy then go pick him up but start the whole thing late for some reason."

"Who is it?" I want to know.

"The kid brother of the boss's son's wife, the one who passed," Eddie says back.

"And what am I supposed to do with him?"

"Why don't we get a look at him first." Now you Eddie the Steady?

"I mean, what's he hired for?"

"I told you," Eddie says, "let's have a look."

"How much he paying?"

"Not my business."

"Not what?" I say just to mess with him.

"You heard me, the boss is responsible for that. He pays you, don't he?"

"I bring it in." I gotta remind him?

"You don't think he's capable?"

"How could I know? You called me." But what was this new bum gonna do? Sweep the floors? I do that. Make the deliveries? I do it, too. Collection? And he's not gonna tell the boss what's what because the boss gave him the job. Eddie better have some big plans. Big plans. "You got big plans, Eddie?"

"Hell, you know me."

"We pick him up every day?"

"Beats me. So what, anyway."

"It's a big change and you're just now calling me." Eddie didn't seem to hear me. "All of a sudden," I finished my thought.

"Everything is all of a sudden," he said, and hung up.

Sam Silk

I directed Eddie to go to Overbrook and pick up Monte first on Monday morning. It'd be best, it seemed to me, if this had as little to do with me directly as possible. I didn't care if I was the one who offered to give the kid a job. I also told Eddie to start an hour later than usual. I didn't give him any reason and the idea only came to me when we were on the phone. But this way, by the time they come to pick me up, Harriett will be gone to work, and so will Paul, off for his first day back at the paper. Monday was going to be a day of firsts. I thought it best if we avoided any unpleasant encounters. Sometime Monte would want to apologize to Paul and Paul probably has some things to own up to, but maybe not today. This was my plan for the first day and I hadn't thought beyond it.

Monte, I gather, had had the usual kind of difficulty returning from war. You can't sleep and you wonder why you're alive and all those other kids aren't. Guilt isn't it. You've been damned to life. Naturally, it was a kind of pressure. You can't talk about it. Only at the oddest times. No one could bear to hear what you really need to say. Words won't do it. That's why they made all those war movies around 1945 so that G.I.s wouldn't have to try to describe it, the indescribable. War is indescribable, well, for lucky ones like me, and I don't know what atrocities they committed over there. I never read the articles. I couldn't do it. I came back and here was Silk Industries. I had a family to raise and my father made it easy for me. He gave me responsibility right away, just enough of it, and somehow it came to me to take some night classes at the Wharton School, which I could do on the G.I. Bill. I had an idea: to modernize the business, to take the old family mill and, using the latest marketing and management techniques, expand it as far as it could go. It was an idea.

This kid? The times are totally different, the economy especially. The city is stagnant. There's no work for black or white kids. Maybe the black ones should be getting their day, but what are they getting? A war zone. And Rizzo won't even let them have that. But Monte's got other troubles, or one thing has compounded the next. He was a sensitive kid and Vietnam must have burned him up. He deployed late because of his age. People don't talk about that much, but if you go in at the right time, believing in it, as we all believed in destroying Hitler and saving Europe, you can handle it. It's a little dose of inoculation. And the ones who die die believing. And the ones injured are heroes, even if only for a minute. Only one time Charles and I talked about the war and in those days it was a little harder for a black man to serve in the Navy than the Army, and he said he served to prove his own valor, to himself and to the country. He had a purpose, in other words. What purpose, Monte, in a shameful war, bodies burning up, and the peaceniks, I don't know if Paul was ever involved in it, burning flags. People have no idea what they do to each other.

Why bother even explaining it? I had to try to give Monte a chance. I wish I had done it earlier. But he wouldn't have wanted it. Three years ago he wouldn't have agreed, as he has now, to work there. I don't blame him. What's happened in those three years or so, I don't know. His poor sister died and he got into drugs. That's what they say. I don't know if he's into drugs. Does anyone know that for a fact? Was he stoned when he robbed Paul? I don't know if he'll be able to work, but why hasn't anyone else tried? Monte, the greatest student Harriett ever had. Who can judge Charles and Anita? And all they've been through. Dammit. It seems to me his life lies in the balance.

Louis Turner

This one comes out of the house real slow, like he's keeping his own time, you know like he's the only critter on earth. Lives up here in Overbrook so he must think he's some kind of Wilt Chamberlain. He's tall and skinny, all bones, but he ain't no Stilt. Hands in his pockets and I say to Eddie, "The dog looks like he lost his bone."

"Shush it," he says. "What you worried about?"

"Keepin' the cash flowing, you know what I mean?"

"Move your ass over, then."

He's standing there at my side door and I'm sitting there and don't he see there's another door on the other side? Not like his block is jammed up with traffic. Go around. I wave my hand but I'm not rolling down the window. "Move your ass over," Crazy Eddie says again.

"Do I ever sit on that side?"

"Maybe you do today." That old man voice.

"Behind the boss?"

"So?"

"It's a mistake." Shit. Isn't it obvious?

"Open the damn door, fool. Or sit up here for now."

I offer up Stilt my hand. White man's handshake. For fuck's sake, he goes for it.

"Monte," Stilt mumbles.

"What's that?"

Stilt doesn't look up. "It's a mistake," I say to Eddie. Then, after Eddie starts rolling up towards the boss's house, I say, "That's Mr. Eddie, driving. When he's not driving, he's the boss and then I'm driving. Call me Louis."

"Call him Louis," Eddie says, repeating me, as if he's the preacher on the pulpit. The kid is looking down, as if he's shy or scared or something. I can't deal with anyone being scared.

"Put on some soul until we get to the boss's house," I lean forward from my new seat and over into the front, and tell Eddie. He's got to listen to me cause he wants me to shut up around Stilt. He thinks I don't know what's what, but I got nine years on him. Hell. "Turn it up so that we can hear without straining our ears here in the back. Ain't that right? Stilt says it's too early in the morning to strain his ears." Long as Eddie does this, which he does, I can sit back and pull out my comic books. I hand one to the kid. "You can read, can't you?" I mean, what was that expression? Like he's drugged or something. Looking at me but not looking at me, far away, almost like into eternity. Once I had a girlfriend all into being Buddhist or Hindu or something, and she had all these pictures of these gods, and some had elephant noses and tusks, but they weren't like real elephant trunks, more like fat snakes, and they had the same expression as this kid right here. "What do they call you, Krishna or something?" I say to him as Eddie fidgets with the dial.

"What? You say something?"

"They call you Krishna, or what?" "Huh? Monte." He says this loud, in case I'm hard of hearing.

"Krishna."

He puts down the comic book, the second issue of *Black Goliath*, on the seat between us and doesn't say nothing. Just looks down at his hands.

Paul Silk

Only on the train, heading to work on my first day, did I finally understand the spit was meant for me, me alone. I was the one who took you from him. He was the one who went to Vietnam, not me. He went because I didn't and you weren't there, there's no separating these things, there's no pretending otherwise. But hadn't Monte been picked up this morning by my father's driver and taken in a car to a job neither he wanted, nor, apparently, the company needed? I was on the run-down train with pickled seats and that I'd had to walk nearly a mile just to catch. And hadn't Monte assaulted me, taken my money, spit in my eye? His spit was hatred. Did I have to accept?

On the train, by the window, as the half-mangled city rolled by, I double-checked myself, searching for the resentment I must be feeling, that I couldn't feel. Was it on account of you, Charlene, that I could never find it? That because of your suffering I could never disparage your brother, even when he deserved it. "It's Monte…" Monte, special creature only a god could create, a moody but powerful deity one must worship whose less noble characteristics are to be accepted, even lauded for their evidence of humanity? We are, after all, to see ourselves in the gods. Or is it, now triple-checking, because I am relieved it's him and not me that I'm afraid to confront the terror of wondering if, as you all but said in delirium last April 24, so near the end that ran up on us before we even—just three days before you died, the last thing you said, we missed Monte's memorial. But why did you think that? What gave you the idea? It won't stop beating against my head, this question.

Double-, triple-checking, wasn't I avoiding a different question I hadn't yet bothered to ask? Why did I accept this job I hardly wanted? What weakness resulted in my taking a temporary, "soft" beat, and reporting nonetheless? Years ago, I said I never wanted to be a reporter again. Charlene, dogged seeker of truth, you would be the reporter, and I would edit, assemble, arrange. The train came to a stop mid-track for no obvious reason, and there, out the window, behind a hurricane fence, prisoners (as I imagined they must have been) in two lines of six men, were doing jumping jacks. If I shut my eyes I could hear the clap of their hands.

The new editor I'd been assigned, Stan Woszek, wore oversized glasses and combed his greasy hair across his wide Baltic head. He'd been hired recently from the *New York Daily News*. "Why, if in fact they are, are people feeling so patriotic in anticipation of the Bicentennial?" His directive was to try to answer that question. I am to cover the city, and somebody else the suburbs. Really, what he meant was, "Why, with all the unemployment and distrust and racial conflict and Nixon and Vietnam was anyone feeling good about the USA?" Was it only to forget? But he didn't want anything too serious. "For example, what's with all the flags all over Kensington?"

That was the kind of question I had to ponder. Is your block organizing a party, or perhaps a concert in the local park? What does the Bicentennial mean to you? Are you aware of the major events, the planned speeches, parades, displays of colonial crafts and games? The train entered Suburban Station. I followed the other commuters up to the street and made my way to my new desk in the newsroom. Crossing in front of the City Hall Annex gave me a strange feeling of elation. What was it with this dour place that nonetheless awakened me? The pale yellow and blue of the art deco details on the Market Street National Bank, whisper tones like the inside of a seashell, as real and natural and distant as the sound of the ocean when you hold the shell to your ear, the building itself, pink as the sand of some far-away desert. No, there was nothing like this in Denver.

In the newsroom some old colleagues came over to welcome me back. One apologized that I couldn't have my old desk. Several wanted me to know how sorry they were.

"You look tired," someone else said, "as if you haven't slept in weeks."

"It isn't more sleep I need," I said to the new colleague, and she smiled.

"Of course," she replied, somehow knowing, "you want to get to work."

Most everyone wanted to talk about the recall campaign, now accelerating because of the city's dire fiscal state, which Rizzo had tried to hide during the election. The campaign had to obtain 145,000 signatures by June 15. It occurred to me that such a democratic movement wouldn't have happened in any other year. The Bicentennial itself was causing resistance against Rizzo.

The editor, Stan, handed me a sheet with some deadlines. Apparently, he had a schedule worked up for these stories, alternating city and suburb all the way to July 4. I admired his foresight. He knew what he wanted. The city stories, he suggested, might alternate white and black. "Is it so simple?" I asked. He didn't answer.

"What about Chinatown or the Barrio?"

"It's up to you. In this city it seems there's almost nothing too obscure."

On my new desk: a Smith-Corona, a stapler, a dictionary, a jar of pencils, and a telephone. There was also a flip calendar, on January, and a stack of old clippings. Apparently the guy who used to work this desk covered the society beat. "Grace Kelly makes surprise visit at the wedding of…" This article, with photographs of Grace Kelly and the bride and groom, was at the top of the pile. Date June 4, 1974.

The telephone. I hated to use the phone. This one was black, with push buttons. I lifted the cord and dropped it. It fell like a broken heart.

I couldn't do this reporting by hiding behind the receiver. How quickly the ideology raised itself, like a weapon. You had to go out and see for yourself. The phone is the most important tool to the journalist. More than one editor had said it: I was a carpenter who refused to use the hammer. I began listing neighborhoods, the places most likely to offer me the best examples of this irrational patriotism. White and black. Little by little the names of places came back to me, Cedar Park, Burlholme, Hawthorne, Eastwick, Olney, the Devil's Pocket, Sharswood, Swampoodle. I had the feeling that I couldn't ever understand this place that was inside of me, and you, too.

Jeanette Johnson

The first day of anything is always the hardest. Maybe it just takes me a while to adjust. It might not seem obvious but I'm a little shy. I'm also the kind of person who likes to be prepared. I don't want to forget anything. And so on the first day of my new job in the Center City office of Dr. Fishman, the dentist, I set my alarm for six so that I could be on the trolley at seven-ten and into work at eight. I even looked over the route from City Hall station to the office. It's only a five-minute walk. I don't want to be late! Dr. Fishman liked me so much after our interview that he suggested I could move up one day from receptionist and file clerk to dental hygienist. He would even pay the tuition for the classes I would need to take.

At six I got out of bed and went to the bathroom to wash up. After my brother went off to Vietnam the bathroom got less busy.

Mama's already gone to work and daddy's up next and brushes his teeth then I get up. Granny uses the bathroom after everyone else has left. But this morning, the first day of a new job, someone is in the bathroom right when I need it. Monte. I knocked, but he didn't respond. "Monte!" I yelled and banged on the door. "Monte get out of the bathroom now, I have to get ready for work." I try not to cuss. I don't like it. And I don't talk like I'm from the ghetto. I'm getting out, anyway. Monte's stuck and they say he's dealing drugs. He seems the same to me as always, only more screwed up in the head because of the war. I hate that war. "Monte! Are you dead?" I could hear the shower running. Nobody's allowed to take long showers in this house but Daddy. "Can't you hear me?" I was so angry I forgot to be nervous for the job.

Finally, he opened the door and poked his wet head out. "What do you think you're doing," I screamed at him. "Getting ready for work," he said in his annoying whisper, smothering his words inside those lips so no one else but him knows what the heck he's saying. I was just close enough to hear, though, come to think of it, the shower was still running. "It's my first day, can't fuck it up. Granny will kill me." I looked at his feet—bony and ugly as Mama's. "Was I supposed to feel sorry for him? Nobody has to threaten me to make me go to work. I want to—so I can move out some day. "Watch your cussing." But, what? I hadn't been home much during the weekend. Since when is my brother going off to work? "Get out of the bathroom!" He tried to tell me he needed more time, but I pushed him away and went in. "You're working all of a sudden and I got to be late? No way." I pushed him out, threw a towel on the floor to soak up his mess, and locked the door. Now I had to hurry. Granny was already up and she poured me iced coffee with sugar and she gave me something to eat, too. I made it and was sitting in the receptionist's chair behind the glass at 7:56. The other lady, who was supposed to train me, hadn't even gotten in yet. That was how I started my first day. The funny thing is it's not even my first first day this week. I went back to the Lebanese place on Saturday night and the boss, whose name I still don't know, came over to me right away and said he wanted me to be one of his dancers. "It's spring," he said, and I kept thinking his ears were going to flap like a flying elephant's, "it's time for a new crop of ladies. Easter's right around the corner." He said if I came back after work on Friday he'd get his best dancer to train me.

12.

Betty Locks Herself in the Bathroom

Betty Silk

I lose track of time lately and the girl isn't very reliable. She only knows when it's time to quit. She brought in a lady, didn't even give me any warning. I gave both of them an angry look. Who was the lady? I looked at my watch. I twisted the diamond on my finger. Someone gave me that ring. I guard it like a hawk.

"Wait a minute," I said and I asked the girl to take me to the bathroom. But the lady said she would take me. It was after five and time for the girl to go. At least now I knew what time it was. The lady told me to get up, let's go to the bathroom. She said it just like that, like a real general. I told her I don't take orders. Who was she? Can I tell you I was afraid for my life? What did she want to take me to the bathroom for? I'll do it myself. But she followed right behind, like a snake. Why was this lady so angry? What had I done to her? I tried to remember. My Abe was sweet as sugar, treated me like a queen. This lady was angry about something. She hasn't said very much and every time she looks at me I frown. She smiles but it isn't a real smile. I thought I should have a sharp knife from the kitchen. Then I saw the girl—she's hard to miss. I asked her if she was afraid. "Afraid of what, missus?" she responds. Of the very mean lady, I don't know what she wants. Take me to the bathroom, I need you to take me.

I whispered it so the lady wouldn't hear. I wanted to put my hand to her ear so she could hear me but I couldn't reach. But she didn't care. She said Harriett was going to take me to the bathroom and then she shut the door. She left.

Harriett is always going through my papers looking for something. That's why I have the girl hide everything in the drawer. She can't have the diamond. Abe gave it to me on my sixtieth birthday. The lady grabbed me hard. She has very strong and cold hands. When she stepped out of the bathroom, I locked the door. I bought that figurine of the girl holding the comb, brushing her long hair. The best porcelain. I checked the door. It's still locked.

Harriett Silk

I left school and drove over to the Lebanon Arms to pay Betty's bills. She's getting worse. At Thanksgiving she knew who everyone was and she could make conversation, especially if it was about Abe and the old days. She's never let go of Abe, I'll give her that. He gave her everything—furs, diamonds, a month at the shore.

From Betty's I still had to go to the Acme, so I hoped to make this a quick visit. Say hello, fix her something from the kitchen if the girl hadn't, and go through the mail and the bills. The girl was already on her way out when I got there. She had her coat on and was sitting near the door in an old chair with an embroidered cushion that no one is supposed to sit in. I'm not even sure it could hold her weight. She had a bag of food. Probably things she grabbed out of the refrigerator. She must have been anxious to get out of there, regardless. Betty was agitated. I draped my coat over a kitchen chair and went over to her sitting near the window in the living room, the radiator right next to her hissing, as if it was the middle of winter.

"Hi Betty," I said, "have you been outside today? Spring is coming."

I was already thinking about getting out of that roasting apartment and what I needed from the grocery store, but I went on as if talking to a child. I told her about Easter break coming, Sam hiring Monte at the mill, and Paul's new position at the paper. I apologized for not stopping at the bakery for the cookies she likes, but she only shrugged, twisting her ring around and around.

"Betty! It's me, Harriett," I said after a while, and I reminded her I had to pay the bills. Did she know who I was? The girl was still there and I asked her if Betty had been like this recently.

"She's a little forgetful."

"Does she need the bathroom?"

The girl said, "It's probably a good idea" and she offered to take her. But I said I would do it and that she could go home if she wished. Betty was already up out of the chair and I came over to her and took her arm to keep her steady.

"Who are you?" she demanded. Betty was a reserved, gentle woman, rarely upset. I told her I was her daughter-in-law Harriett and I was going to take her to the bathroom. Abe, she said, was "sweet as honey."

"Of course he was, I remember," I said. "I miss him, too."

"Who are you?" she asked again, and then, as we neared the hallway and the turn to the bathroom, she asked, in a dreamlike voice, as if she were talking in her sleep, "Whose son is Paul?"

"My son, the son of Sam and me." The question was a relief. It had some relation to reality.

But then, in a different, belligerent tone, she said, "No he's not. He can't be."

She pushed my hand away and went over to the girl, who was halfway out the door, and tried to whisper something in her ear. The girl pretended not to hear.

Betty went the opposite way from the bathroom and into the kitchen. Was she looking for something? I had to follow and turn her around and lead her back toward the bathroom. "Do you want help?" I asked, with as much kindness as I could muster. The woman was testing my patience.

If only that was all. She went inside the bathroom and as I tired to keep the door open to see if she wanted my help, she pushed it shut and locked it. Now my mother-in-law was locked in the bathroom.

At first I begged her to unlock the door. She ignored me. "Abe was an angel," she said, and then, strangely, knocked on the door as if she was the one trying to get in. Hopeful this meant she wanted to get out, or was merely playing a game, I knocked back and said, "Are you all right?" Trying the gentlest possible voice, I told her how to unlock the door and open it.

Then she said, "A lady is trying to steal my money," by which she must have meant me.

"She isn't trying to steal your money," I responded immediately. "I promise you, now please unlock the door."

"She comes here when I'm not looking and shuffles all the papers."

In the kitchen I dialed Sam at the mill. He was still there. "I'm not going to break down the door," I told him. He suggested I go down the hall and get Harry. "And what's he going to do, tell her off-color jokes? She'll never come out. She's your mother. I'll sit outside the bathroom, grade papers, and talk to her. Make sure she's still alive. You get over here now and get her out."

Louis Turner

I pull into the courtyard where we keep the delivery van. Dionne Warwick is playing. Every time she comes on I feel a little softer and I think, "Louis," turn the dial, "she's gonna melt you, Eddie's gonna come out and find a puddle in the driver's seat. But she is all I got. Every other station is going on about Rizzo. They want to kick him out. Can they do that? I know a brother who voted for him. That's crazy, but not as crazy as Eddie grabbing onto the door handle and saying we got to go, in the car, to rescue the boss's mama locked in the bathroom. "What? It's time to kick back."

"We got to go," he says.

"You go. I'm hopping on the El."

"Boss is already in the car," Eddie insists.

"What about Krishna?"

"Who?"

"Shit, Eddie. The new Manager of Operations."

"What you talking about, Louis, the lady's locked in the bathroom.

We're all going. Boss says in case one of us can't get the door open the other will."

"Call the super. That's what they do on T.V."

"She's scared, fool."

All right, just a minute. Now we're back in the car, but this time I'm in my own seat behind Eddie and Krishna's behind the boss. I don't want anybody messing with my head.

Now here's what I'm expecting: an old lady with five teeth and hair all what's way screaming and kicking the door and a fire engine downstairs with the siren going. I mean, the whole works. But the boss opens the door to the apartment and it's like a library or something. Lights are off like no one lives there and after a while we find the boss's wife sitting in a chair reading. I don't hear a lady screaming. Is she dead? Because if this is no library maybe it's a funeral parlor. But damn, the view.

The boss talks to his wife. She's taller than he is. I never knew that. But then I never see her. I've only been in their kitchen a few times. She tells him what's up and thanks us all for coming. She looks at Krishna a long time like she's his mama. I don't know where he's looking. The boss is upset and he's talking to his mama through the door. Does he believe the wife? He thinks she is dead, too. No, she's alive.

"What she saying?" I ask Eddie. He's up real close looking at the lock, jiggling it, like it might come loose. I'm not jumping in there unless the boss says.

"A lady's stealing her money, that's what she's saying."

"So why'd she lock herself in there?"

Eddie doesn't say. He just says the lock isn't a standard lock. He thinks she locked a slide bolt, too. And he says the super's out. We might have to wait.

"Nah, that's why we're here."

I nod to the boss's wife and smile and I go up to the bathroom door real quiet. I know how to talk to old grannies. "Missus," I say, "I got the lady who's stealing from you. I took her away. You can come out now. It's safe."

She's scratching around in there like a sad dog. I get myself teared up because the lady's not right. "I'm washing up," she says. "My hands are dirty."

"It's safe. The lady, she's gone. They took her away."

"Who are you?"

"Missus, I'm Louis. I work for your son, Mr. Silk."

"My husband Abe?"

"No, ma'am. Sam, your son. He's here, too. He's here next to me."

"Abe built this house, that's how good he was. Sir? Is your skin black? I can tell."

This makes me laugh. The lady's funny. "Oh, I'm black all right. Black as night. I'm the black angel. Now your supper's almost ready and we're gonna sit down."

Everyone's crowded around the door trying to see what I'm doing. They're chirping, "Listen to Louis!" I swat them away. Give me room to work! This all Louis. "Give him a chance," the boss says to Eddie.

"I don't like you," the lady says and she kicks the door. "Never have." She says it just like that.

"I know I'm beautiful." That's what I say.

"You're ugly." She kicks again.

Eddie pulls me away. "Now you got her agitated," he says. A minute ago I was the hero.

Krishna's just hanging back, the whole time not saying anything. Been like this all day. "You gonna just stand there?" He nods, comes up to the door, feels the door with his hand—long, bony fingers, presses on it like the doctors do on TV examining a pregnant woman, feeling around to make sure all the parts are there. They can tell if the baby's healthy or not just by pressing. Like seals. Still, nothing coming out of his mouth. I can't hear the lady either. Then he asks the boss to see what's in the toolbox we brought over from the mill. We already tried to unscrew the cover and look inside the lock. Then Krishna goes back over to the door, feels around again. My stomach growls. The boss's wife is up there with him, yapping away. She only talks to him, barely to the boss. The boss is on the phone. I think he's trying to call the super again.

Krishna's pressing. He says something to the boss's wife. "He thinks the slide bolt's open," Eddie says. You know it is. Because I told her it was safe. Only she got distracted and started washing her hands. Can't make sense of old people!

The boss's wife goes away for a minute and comes back with a manila folder. She hands it to Krishna and he slides it in the doorjamb. "We already tried a charge card," Eddie says, but real quiet, like he doesn't mean to. Krishna's bent down, his nose to the door handle. He slides the folder and presses, with the tips of his fingers, against the door handle, like a kid touching a tit for the first time. He pulls the manila folder out then slides it up instead of down. He's whistling now, real loud. But I want to know what's she saying? She cursing him out? "Is the water running?" I say.

"Why you want to know that?" Eddie answers. He's always answering a question with a question.

"She still washing her hands?"

"You see me here? I ain't in there with her!"

"Never mind."

"The kid's working," he says, like it's a secret to be let in on.

"Yeah and the boss is on the phone. What's new?"

"Keep it quiet, please," the boss's wife says, one word at a time, real slow. What is this, English class? But that was it, as if her command did it. We didn't even hear it because Krishna opened the door slow, I mean gentle. That dog's got no problem with the ladies. He opened that door just a little at first and then granny gave out a sigh, like she'd been caught doing something ugly, and everyone stepped back to make room. The boss came up, took her arm and led her into the living room. The boss's wife turned on the lights. And just like that we were in a golden palace and I was standing on a Chinese carpet.

13.

Paul's Discovery

Paul Silk

I began to jot down some notes. The articles would have to have a theme, something to connect them beyond "neighbors celebrate the Bicentennial." If that was going to be the concept the articles will be quickly forgotten, if they would even be read at all. So why bother?

Suddenly I had the feeling that I needed to see everything, everywhere. Not the totality of the city, but the parts. Each block, one at a time. This idea excited and frightened me. Would it be possible? Could someone walk every block in every neighborhood, in and out of worlds? No, no, that couldn't be the way to do this. I have to ask around. I have to start to ask. One thing might lead to another.

You would say to me, "You love the city because it's a little sick and because you know it's imperfect. The less perfect it is, to you the more real. And what isn't perfect can be loved even more intensely, it can be stroked, smoothed, fixed." Charlene, you on the other hand wanted things perfect. A word, a sentence, a paragraph, a story, a city. Ours was so imperfect we had to leave. Your mind was too sharp. It couldn't smooth things over and so every imperfection was like a tripwire and each one stung.

Trying to figure my Bicentennial stories I went over to the giant map in the newsroom. Did I squint more than usual, as if I couldn't bear it? Couldn't we look together, across the city? And see? People certainly feeling strained. You would say, "And quite specifically, white and black people, both." "And differently," I would say. Doesn't everyone want to celebrate the Bicentennial? Don't they want to feel good about their country, but most of all their city? And yet there are reasons they can't and those reasons gnaw at them, they eat away at their imaginations. So they only hope to avoid disaster. They decide to keep things small, "manageable." They decide to keep it safe and close. Fear has done this, but the editor doesn't want me to write about fear.

The opposite of fear, Charlene? Is it freedom? Isn't that anyway what's being celebrated? Philadelphia freedom? A delicious kind of thing, it should be. What would you say? The challenge will become apparent almost immediately, won't it? Freedom for white people, isn't it the freedom to choose to not live with black neighbors? "White flight," isn't this freedom? And for black people: freedom not to be harassed, freedom not to be hated: the freedom not to be denied freedom. This, too, is a negative freedom. Where will I find that boundless freedom, the freedom that doesn't deny others their own? Can I find it in 1976, in Philadelphia? Where will I look? How will I know it when I see it?

Of course I recalled standing here in front of the map, in that same spot, late one evening not even ten years ago. Hardly anyone was left in the newsroom at that hour. You had stayed because you worked the hardest and I was waiting for you to finish up. You came over and stood by me in front of the map. I had no idea then that we would leave.

No, in fact I was searching for something particular, the exact right place for us to live after the wedding, for I was convinced that it existed. I was convinced because it had to be so. Well, I was sure of it. And with you, for once, I wanted everything to be perfect.

In those days our love was a shared secret. Only a few knew. You held my hand in front of the map, as we were virtually alone in the newsroom, and I had the sense of floating in that giant building. Such strength it gave me to hold your hand. Anyone who looked into your steel eyes must have felt the strength. "I'm looking for a place for us to live," I admitted. You must have known already that it couldn't be. That place wouldn't be in Philadelphia. But your strength gave you such patience. You could wait without demanding anything.

You acquiesced and for a few days we went walking all around the city. Walking from one neighborhood to the next gave me a sense of freedom I'd never felt before, a sense that the city was infinite, a sense of my own future. I saw, at last, how people had given themselves to the city. I saw all the little ways, the decorations, flags, flowers, the additions they'd built, themselves perhaps, or with the help of a neighbor, sometimes skillfully, sometimes dreadfully. The city awakened in their hands as they wanted or as they could afford. What a feeling this gave me, a sad, gentle feeling, a wash of weakness. Everyone must try to master the city, but no one can.

What were you thinking when we set off from your house in Overbrook? That my enthusiasms, if let go long enough, would peter out? That I'd lose my bearings? My dear Charlene, you were never manipulative. You waited to judge, and all my life I've been surrounded by judgmental women. You didn't have to interfere, you didn't want to just then. Perhaps you weren't sure yet. But once you made up your mind…

It was warm, but not hot, October maybe. Granny made us sandwiches and you put them in your bag. We smiled, conspiring. We'd planned to find some corner bar or cafe in some neighborhood we didn't yet know. It was part of the game. We didn't want to tell Granny of our plans.

The walk across the city was a test. You wanted to know, to feel it in your bones, where we might be welcome. "Not accepted, Paul, not tolerated," you said. You doubted I really understood. To find this out, we'd have to go inside drug stores, luncheonettes, little groceries, walk down narrow blocks where front porches kiss each other from across the street, testing the peering eyes. "How will you know?" I asked.

"I'll know instantly," you replied. You were playing along, but you weren't insincere.

We had all day. We would walk as much as our feet would let us. If the trolley came and we wanted to make up some ground? Sure. We could also use the bus and the El. That day we made it all the way from Overbrook to the Northern Liberties before things turned sour.

I recall we got to the corner of 36th and Powelton rather quickly. Did we take the trolley right away, is that why in my memory we got there immediately? We didn't need to walk through Overbrook and West Powelton, you said, there was no point. Right away, I felt at home there. But Powelton Village, you knew because you had contributed to a story, "Where Integration Drives Up Home Values." "Look up at the turrets, domes, belvederes, gables—"

"Say what?" you said, laughing.

"Look up."

"No, that word. Please! Say it again."

"What? Dome?"

"Not that one, silly man. The other one."

"Turret."

"No, baby."

"Gable."

"You're doing this on purpose."

"Belvedere?"

"Yes! Say it again."

"Belvedere?"

"What does it mean?" Your eyes got wide, Charlene.

"It's that little room—at the top of that house, a look-out, so you can see far. You can watch your ships go out to sea." The sky is a fantasy, like a children's fable—that must be a good sign. "People aren't stuck around here in their old ways of thinking."

How long did we stand on that corner, turning in circles? Did I start to hum? "You sound like Grandpa did after his stroke. When Granny would bring him iced coffee. He'd look at it and groan just like that, wouldn't even need to drink it, that's how happy he was," you said. This is the kind of thing we would say to each other in the early days, when each new thing was revealed.

I remember now, standing there, a conversation about brick. I pointed out the thin, oblong, orange brick of the houses on the one corner and the traditional red brick of the houses on the corner opposite. I said I liked the orange better because it was less traditional and because it captured the light. "The orange brick will glow golden in the morning or the evening, depending." You disagreed. You refused to acknowledge that brick should be anything but red.

"It's called red brick for a reason."

"Not orange brick?" All time and space existed in that instant on that corner.

I pointed out the elementary school across the street. Would we send our children here one day? The schoolyard was filled with children. We closed our eyes to listen and then we crossed the street to see. I mentioned that black and white children were playing together. You didn't answer. Were you trying to picture your child, our child, on that playground? Charlene, did you ever picture our child, black and white? "Am I ready?" I said, then. "I don't know if I'll ever be ready." Did you ever ask what I thought? But maybe you knew and you couldn't bear to say it. I wanted a child, our child. But when you said, "I don't know if I'll ever be ready," I said, "OK." I said, "I'll be patient and wait to find out."

How long did we stand in front of the Powell School watching the children play?

We crossed one of the bridges over the Schuylkill. It might have been the Walnut Street Bridge, the bridge from which Mr. Rizzo once threatened to throw "hippies and faggots" into the river. He was only police chief then, but we felt his eyes on us and we held hands even tighter crossing the bridge. The longer we held hands like that the more we felt at risk. We sat for a while in the Rittenhouse Coffee Shop. We held hands there, too, and listened to an old recording of Woody Guthrie. "This land is our land." I ate a piece of cake and you ate nothing. You yawned. It was a weekday and we had both managed to get the day off. I didn't want to rush. I avoided talking about 36th and Powelton and the little terrace of the apartment on the third floor I had noticed that could some day be ours. But something wasn't right, as if you had seen through everything—all time and space—and nothing was really what it seemed.

A little while later, in the bright warm sun we stood on the sidewalk in front of the Trocadero, its faded marquee still advertising "Burlesque Continuous 11AM to Midnight." A breeze blew the stench from a fish market on the corner. We had stopped there on the way to Olde City and we ate one of Granny's sandwiches. I had a vague idea. What if we lived in a place like this, "someone else's place," neither white nor black, then it wouldn't matter. But how could we? The stench alone. "You like it half dead, half alive," you said. "That's what appeals to you. That isn't what appeals to me."

You didn't like it there or in Olde City. But at least there I could point to construction workers renovating the shipping warehouses and machine shops. At the intersection of two tiny alleys we tried to distinguish the various sounds: a typewriter, a machine belt, a man arguing with another man over the price of a coffee, a seagull, and a woman singing. We couldn't understand the words. She might have been singing in Yiddish. "We could create our own world here, build it from red brick, wood, cobblestone, and rust," I said, sadly and hopefully.

You pushed me under a brick archway between two buildings. You kissed me and said, "I love you but I'm not going to live here."

Not sure what I was thinking, we walked along the tenderloin into Northern Liberties. I'd heard it was a tolerant place, the opposite of Kensington. Old Eastern European families, Jews, five generations of Negro families all lived here in harmony. And yet, was this the 19th century? I half expected horse carts filled with coal or wood, a pack of goats on the way to the slaughterhouse. The sun had dipped below the buildings and the air was turning cool. You crossed your arms to keep warm. You wouldn't let me hold you. We went inside a hardware store but the place was so jammed with boxes, crates piled high, bags of nails, screws, nuts and bolts. Someone was upstairs, his feet creaking the ceiling. Was it going to cave in? Then I turned and a small, blistered woman behind the counter asked what we needed. "Izzy will be down in a minute," she said. "Are you one of the new ones? I'll give you a hint, don't go into the joint on the corner." She smiled. She was doing us a favor.

Outside, I took you in my arms. You allowed it for a minute and once more I let myself dream. I could have you and we could live here happily, in peace. "The time is now to straighten up Girard College,"

I said in your ear, in my best Martin Luther King, the words he had said that morning we first met. I don't know if even for a moment you appreciated it because it was then, just then, that a policeman tapped me on my shoulder.

"No sir, not on my beat," he said.

This was the second time. You stepped away quickly, straightened yourself, and you apologized to the officer. It didn't matter to you, Charlene, you had already decided. All that was left were formalities, finding a new job and telling our parents. But I couldn't bear to hear you talk like this. "No love on your beat, then. Only hate," I said.

The policeman was twice my size. He wore black leather gloves, Nazi gloves. I wanted to tell you they were Nazi gloves. "Paul, shush," you said.

"Listen to the lady," he said. "Now, you go that way and she goes this way. I stand here and watch."

"That isn't possible," I said. "We're going to the same place."

He put his hands on your shoulders.

"You're molesting a newspaper reporter!" I cried.

"That's right, you're going to the same place," he said, ignoring me. He shoved you in the patrol car and slammed the door. "The same place," he said, and he put his arm out like an usher at the movies.

We spent two hours at the station house. After a while they let me dial Albert and he made some calls and they let us go.

What could I do then? We were hungry and tired. You said you wanted to go into the paper, you had leads to follow, and I agreed to go too. In silence, we got on the El. At City Hall, we got off the car and started walking along the platform. I walked down the platform to the subway north thinking you were behind me. But you had kept going, up the next staircase to the street. You were going to walk. We arrived in the newsroom at the same time and we went in opposite directions to our desks.

My desk now isn't far from yours though the room has been rearranged to accommodate more reporters. It's loud in here, but newsroom buzz is like a motor of its own. I grabbed my jacket off the back of my chair and went walking, on a hunt for stories of freedom.

It occurred to me to start at the beginning, 40th and Lancaster, where we met waiting for Dr. King to come on. You had come down on the trolley that morning, a short ride from 63rd and Lebanon that probably took ten minutes, maybe less. It took me an hour today. There was track work in the tunnel, "in preparation for the Bicentennial." That day, in 1965, I tried to tell you how much I liked the trolley. "This is how human beings should travel," I said, but you weren't interested. "Slowly, and at a reasonable speed." You had to get to that freshman orientation. Now here I was standing outside the storefront church that must have been originally a bank, with columns and a clock over the door. "Come in, come in," a man leaned out the door and spoke to me. Can you see it, Charlene?

"It's all right, thank you!" How could I say I am allergic to religion? But what kind of journalist in search of stories dismisses someone? I kept walking up the Avenue, surely more weary than it was a decade before. The movie house was gone, the Sun Ray, the Woolworth's, only a tangle of corner stores, money lenders, pawn shops, and men floating around the corners, in and out of the shadows. I stood at a lunch counter, swimming pool tiles on the floor. Filthy tiles, the fabric covers of the stools torn, taped, torn again. A Korean woman poured me a coffee. I asked her what's happening in the neighborhood for the Bicentennial. Any parties, street fairs, festivals? "No parties," she said, and smiled, "only work."

A block further, at Fairmount Avenue, I began to notice a pattern: bars, delis, and restaurants on the corners, variety, hardware, clothing mid-block. Maybe the basic structure of the city would hold, despite the rupturing, eternal, immutable? I met a slender white woman getting out of a car. "You live around here?" She was going into a dance studio on the second floor of an old Kresge. "Performing for the Bicentennial?" Yes, she said, but in New York.

So it went, Charlene. Another half hour and I had nothing more than a track on a children's performance at the zoo. The trolley heading east approached. I let it go by. School let out and fourteen-year-old boys ravaged the street. I ducked inside the Liberty Bell Store. The upstairs windows are boarded up, painted, and used to advertise what's inside. "Toys," "Bikes," "Dolls," "Hobbies," "Games." A sign posted inside: "The Oldest Black-Owned Toy Store in Philadelphia, Established 1938." A man in a tweed jacket approached. "You need a bike for your little girl?" he asked, with a vaguely aristocratic accent. His eyes gleamed. They brightened still when I mentioned the Bicentennial. He handed me a card, "Old Philadelphia Association," J.M. Fiske Sr., President. This was Mr. Fiske. The Association is located on South 6th Street. "We're all descendants of the first free Negroes of this city."

I thought about this. "I'm impressed."

"Goes back longer than the Declaration of Independence. We keep meticulous record." Can you hear the quality of his voice, Charlene?

I arranged to meet him there, at the Association office, next week. The store was as meticulous as its owner. There were, in fact, aisles of toys, bikes, dolls, hobbies, and games. Then near the cash register, a pretty yellow painted table with sweaters, neatly folded. "$12.50 each." Sweaters? Light blue, in crew neck and v-neck, with dark blue stripes. The same in brown and orange, green and black. Silk Line sweaters, circa? Charlene, you could say exactly, you remember. Maybe 1970. One of these came by mail to Denver.

I thanked Mr. Fiske, reconfirmed our meeting, and left. I crossed the street in front of a westbound trolley, stared at the store from the other side, sun flashing in my eyes. Fiske Toys carries Silk sweaters, at 4087 Lancaster Avenue. I went back inside and found the owner.

"A new line for us," said Mr. Fiske when I asked about the sweaters, and he turned his back on me, walked away.

"It's 1976, I suppose you have to try new things," I said.

"Sir," he called out. "Thank you for the advice."

By three in the afternoon I found myself, after several bus and trolley rides, in front of the Lebanon Arms. My mother had told me that Nana Betty had locked herself in the bathroom. She wouldn't come out until Monte got the door opened. I wondered if she was all right.

I pulled a chair up close to her, near the window. "How can you stand it, it's so hot in here?" I asked but she didn't hear. "You're OK after yesterday?"

"What yesterday?"

"The bathroom."

"A lady," she said, leaning forward, and then she stopped and didn't say more. "You are a beautiful boy."

I told her about my return to the paper. For a moment, it seemed her head had cleared. She appeared to know I had been a reporter before and even an editor. She smiled. The smile never left her face. Encouraged, I told her in detail about the assignment. She raised her eyebrows. I tried to explain that the stories would be about people inventing their own Bicentennial celebrations. "People are excited," I finally said. "It's only a few months away."

"It's a beautiful place," she said, and took my hand. "A beautiful, beautiful place."

Paul Silk

How would you do it, Charlene? Make a list of potential stories, rank them, make exploratory phone calls, expand the list. The more you call the more you learn. I made a list but otherwise I'm in the dark, going by feel. You said I had too much imagination to be a reporter. "You can't stick to the facts! You don't even believe there are facts!" You exaggerated, of course.

I'm relearning the bus system. Don't shake your head. This morning I took a ride on the 47 bus to Olney, the old German neighborhood. Still German, but like everywhere the population is changing. The oldtimers are dying; they post the obituaries on the side of the church, like in the old country. They make pretzels, schnitzel, musical instruments, and their houses have terracotta roofs. Koreans have started moving in, black folks, Puerto Ricans. It won't be long until all the Germans are gone. On 5th Street I found an old German baker. For the Bicentennial he's going to bake and then assemble a fifteen-foot-tall pumpernickel Independence Hall and present it to the neighborhood on July 4 during a block part on Lindley Avenue. Why? "This is the taste of freedom."

I walked down 5th Street. I thought I could walk all the way down-town. At one corner I noticed a poster taped to a pole: *Oppresión: una pieza en 200 años, 28 Junio – 20 Julio, Teatro del Barrio*. I wrote down the number and walked until I came to a stop at Lehigh Avenue in front of a storefront decorated in red, white, and blue bunting with little flags stuck in the pavement. The neon sign said, "Fortunes." "Tarot, palms, tea leaves, crystal ball, which do you want?" I didn't want any, I tried to say. I wanted to know about the Bicentennial, all these flags, all the red, white, and blue. A baby girl all in pink, ruffles, tried to walk across the rug. She kept falling. Her mother, the daughter of the fortuneteller, was pregnant. "This is my Bicentennial baby," she said, and pointed to her stomach. "Due July Fourth. Five dollars for the fortune."

"Tell me the city's fortune," I asked her mother, "the city's Bicentennial fortune. Will everything go wrong?"

The fortuneteller put down her cigarette, picked it up again, and said, "Why you want to know?"

"Everyone wants to know."

"You have small hands, let me see your hand, there's a lot to tell," she said, in a demanding voice.

"Big crowds?" I would start my series off with this, Charlene, a prognostication.

"Sit down, have some water. You're sweating."

"My legs are tired. You're excited for the Bicentennial?"

"The baby!" the medium laughed.

"The flags?"

"Let's look at the hands. The hands tell."

"I don't want to know! I'll pay five dollars for the fortune. Tell me what you're doing for the Bicentennial—"

"Look at her. Having a baby!"

"The city, the Bicentennial city, how does the future hold?" The girl in pink tumbled again. "Look into the crystal ball!"

"Pay first," the daughter demanded.

I paid. The medium dimmed the lights. The bunting rattled against the window. The girl in pink jumped on her mother's lap.

"I don't need the crystal ball to tell you. You already know. I see a snake that is a circle. The Bicentennial is an end and a beginning both."

"That's it?"

"That's everything," she whispered.

"I can't believe it."

"Go next door, Mr. Joe, he'll tell you. He already knows."

"Knows what?"

"You'll find what you need."

I went next door.

"How much did she charge you?" asked Mr. Joe, a little man with olive skin, bags under his eyes, gruff voice.

"Five dollars," I admitted.

"Five dollars!"

"You have a Coke?"

"I got everything you need here. One Coke. Five dollars."

"Five dollars?"

"You're thick, mister. Sit down," he insisted.

I sat, drank the Coke, looked up. There on the shelf, below boxes of light bulbs, Silk Line sweaters. "2 for $10."

"You sell clothing?"

"I sell any and every thing, kid."

"Those are nice sweaters."

"I wear them myself," he said offhandedly.

"I don't understand. Excuse me. Sometimes I get confused. I left this city in 1969. Seems like another time. Your customers come here to buy sweaters?"

"They come here to buy everything, my friend."

"Where do you get them?"

"The sweaters? Now you're asking too many questions. Why don't I ask you something?"

"Go ahead."

"Did she read your fortune?"

"Not exactly."

"That's no answer," he said. He lit a cigarette.

"I asked for something different."

120

"She took you in the back?"

"What do you—"

"No, she don't do that. She's the real thing," he laughed.

"Then I could be a palm reader."

"Oh no, don't say that."

"What happens when you sell all the sweaters? You get more?"

"Yeah, I get more."

"From who?"

"Factory direct."

"I don't get why," I said.

"You a cop? A reporter? You don't seem like either. Seem like you're from another planet."

"Alien reporter."

"Not now." He pushed me out the door.

"Next week?"

"Look, here I am, 2739 North 5th. I ain't moving."

Sam Silk

What was I to do about Monte? Keep him with me? Well, Eddie and Louis never would allow it. But what am I risking? What happened at my mother's only makes it worse. He has the hands of a lover or a killer, I'm not sure which. Maybe Harriett is right about him, he could do anything. If only someone would clear a path. I'd give him Silk Industries if he could save it.

What should I do? Bring him with me to meet with the bank? Now there are two banks on top of what I owe creditors. What does Albert say? Cut your losses. He drew up bankruptcy papers. I wasn't available that day. He came to my house, I gave him a drink. That's when I suggested to him that I just needed a bit more time. No reason to worry. New territories are opening up.

Thank God I never expected Alan or Paul to succeed me. At least they have a chance. I tell myself, if only I can make it to the fall line. We better have one this year. Keep the shopkeepers happy. Send Louis and Eddie to Newark, Baltimore, even Washington, DC. Make the payment. Get some air. People always need sweaters. I can't lose sight of that. Silk Industries has been making them for seventy years.

Monte Johnson

From the Desk of... Monte Johnson

I knew Paul's family owned a big business, "the mill." No, The Mill. And Paul's mom was Mrs. Silk (the woman is a legend) and I even knew The Mill had a name, Silk Industries. This is embarrassing. No, I mean *embarrassing*. I thought they made silk. Of course they made silk, it's the name. Monte Johnson, you've answered incorrectly. But you still win this personalized notepad!

In the shower the morning of my first day, I tried to list all the things made from silk (and a picture of each thing appeared in my head): (1) silk sheets; (2) silk ties; (3) silk ribbon; (4) silk handkerchiefs; (5) silk panties; (6) silk shirts; (7) silk cravats; (8) silk nightgowns. All this silk. Did my sister know it? On her wedding day, opening the presents, did she say to Paul, Where's all my silk, baby? No, that would be Jeanette.

But what do you all do here, if you're not making silk?

You think I know?

You think I don't know what kind of racket this is?

14.

Paul Works His Beat

Paul Silk

I went into the newsroom, wrote and filed the story on the pumper-nickel Independence Hall, and then took the subway down to South Street and walked to the office of the Old Philadelphia Association. I walked on the left side of the street to feel the sun on my face and the warmth and the street jumping all around me. It could have been a magical forest. Even in mid-day it gave off a beat. It carried me, Charlene, and I practically floated into Mr. Fiske's tidy office. Dark wood paneling, a tin ceiling that seemed to hang by a thread, glass light fixtures on long brass rods. "A Jewish delicatessen owned by a family, Finklestein, from Russia. We bought it from their descendants and you want to know why? This was the original Free African Society and I have the papers to prove it. We bought it back, in other words." He wore a bow tie and a checkered shirt.

"A delicatessen," I repeated.

"You've got your eye on the fixtures. They're good enough for us right now. They didn't have electricity back when this was the Free African Society."

"For the Bicentennial, Mr. Fiske, the Society, the Association, your association, you have big plans?"

"More than plans, Mr. Silk, we're going to make a statement."

He asked me to sit down and brought out two old wooden folding chairs with brass hinges. They gave off a slight scent of furniture polish. As I sat down he went over to the old deli case for a pile of books and papers. He returned, straightened himself, cleared his throat, Charlene, almost birdlike, and placed the books on the floor. What was it, the dark room, the scent of the furniture polish, Mr. Fiske's startling self-assurance, "pride beyond pride?" I'm in the room with Mr. Fiske holding in my hand the original papers of the Free African Society. "The men who signed this, look at their names. First of all, what do you see? Dickinson, Hopkinson, Rush. Well, do you know who they are? Signers of the Declaration of Independence. Founding Fathers. And these names here: Allen, Jones, Forten, they are the free Africans, their equals. So we're going to call them, in our Bicentennial program, the Black Founding Fathers. We aren't going out on a limb. The scholars are making the same assessment, Mr. Silk, they've come here to our archive to trace these same associations. These men gave birth to a new way of life, Black Freedom in America, they demanded it and they protected it. They fostered it and they nurtured it. From this room came generations of families, business owners, doctors, publishers, lawyers, builders, teachers, schoolmasters, the greatest chefs, poets, virtuosos on the violin and the harpsichord. All this you comprehend before the slaves were emancipated and before the poor Southerners came this way. We celebrate that distinction. Not without consciousness of our shared fates, mind you, we are hardly naïve or hard of heart, but we were always literate and not nearly so hungry. They began publishing from this very room, declarations of freedom, defiance, and, Mr. Silk, the beauty that only they could know. Long after selling the building to the Russians (peasants probably not any less hungry than the Southerners who had by now overwhelmed the Old Philadelphians with their numbers and their need), they continued to publish works of high literature." Did I understand? He didn't mean for me to answer, breaking the short silence by bending down for a book at the top of his little pile. Only then I noticed his hands shaking slightly. He couldn't help it. But he didn't fumble the book, hardbound, with a sage-colored cloth cover and gold embossing on the spine. *The Book of Dreams* by A.V. Bellis.

"Do you know it? You don't know it. If you don't mind, consider 'Dream of the city of water, smoke, and steam,' from 1921. The book was published in 1923, but this particular poem had been printed earlier, in the literary magazine of Swarthmore College. His grandfather, a Presbyterian minister, descended from a baker who made the bread for the first United States Congress. He was a master orator, put an end to the talk of colonizing blacks in Africa. You see he had a way with words and words protected the Old Philadelphians, though sometimes not well enough. You're a newspaperman, you understand. We celebrate words during the Bicentennial, don't we? Now A.V. Bellis is Reverend Bellis's great-grandson. This is Bellis's great-grandson: 'Above the line you recognize/there is no line,' you see that's how the poem starts. 'Below the line you recognize/only distant mind. The same swell, pulse, and morning/On Vineyard Street as on Water. Before it the sky sent and the river leapt and the fire roared/The turbine whipped and the air/scorched/dripped back/The postman had already paid/The postage. The breath left hot/hit air/marked itself *blanche* for you to see/cold now/the same still. The same swell, pulse, and morning/the steam shoots through pipes/a jet fish eludes the shark. Above the line you recognize/there is no line. Below the line you recognize/only distant mind.' The city is our greatest teacher, Mr. Silk."

"Only humans aren't paying much attention."

"No, it isn't that they aren't paying attention. It's that they don't know what to focus on. They don't have the right teachers. Or they get distracted. The city plays tricks. I would lend you this book but we need it for the exhibition."

"The city plays tricks," I repeated.

"Thank you for stopping by. Call if you need anything more."

"The sweaters, Mr. Fiske? I still don't quite understand."

"A favor to a friend, Mr. Silk. I think I know why you ask. But think of it that way, a favor. I assure you."

I crossed the street into the sun. Children rocked on the seesaw, back and forth, back and forth. Through the open gate I sat on a wooden bench. I needed to scribble notes, record impressions. I didn't know if I wanted to forget the words of A.V. Bellis, in Mr. Fiske's alabaster voice, or swim in them forever. A pool? A sea? A river? And the mouth of A.V. Bellis, the words spilling in and spilling out with the convulsive tide. "A favor."

How long was I there? A mother and an infant sat down next to me. Maybe three or four different mothers. Maybe the same mother the whole time. What if I spend my life digging around, Charlene, what will the city have to say?

Suddenly I got up, closed the notebook, slipped the pencil behind my ear, and walked out. On the way I noticed a poster. "Freedom," it said, would be performed at the Society Hill Playhouse throughout the Bicentennial celebration. The theater was two blocks away. In my confusion I went east on Lombard all the way to 4th. How could I go the wrong way? I collapsed on a bench facing a brick wall and tried to calm myself. The wall said nothing. You, clear as day, said, "Get up!" Your voice, Charlene. I walked fast, sweating from shame. Even still, it was an eternity to get to 8th Street. Then I went left toward South instead of right. Where is it? I entered a pawnshop and asked. "Behind you," said the little man behind counter. "All you got to do is turn around."

Susan Painter

I wasn't ready for him, I just wasn't ready for him. We were rehearsing the scene of Armon, the protagonist, being swept up in a stormy sea. It's a metaphor inside a metaphor, of a terrible dream. The dream of freedom isn't an easy dream! But Kevin, the actor playing Armon, was acting the idea of a stormy dream. He was pretending. He wasn't feeling the storm. He wasn't inside the storm and the storm wasn't inside him. Armon isn't trying to have a nightmare and he isn't fighting it either because he's asleep and his mind, though it's creating all these images and actions, is at rest. Let yourself go! I got up on the stage and lay down and I closed my eyes to demonstrate. And I felt the wind of a terrible dream. My terrible dream is always the same, of my father dying in the war, in France, and not meeting my mother in Paris, and therefore me not even or ever existing and I let that dream get started in my mind at rest and felt it run through me, top to bottom, bottom to top, the most frightening, perplexing, and also unnaturally calming dream, because nothing anymore was expected of me. The most freedom there is! I didn't say all this to Kevin. You have to give actors one instruction at a time and then the next and then the next, like putting on your underwear and then your shirt and then your coat. You can't put all this on at the same time.

I got up from the stage lightheaded with tears forming in my eyes and my body heavy, heavy and light, this was the perfect metaphor for the stormy sea. You won't find freedom unless you survive it. I looked up into the darkness of the theater, with the chalky light dancing above the seats, and he was there at the back, and even from far away I could tell he was uncomfortable. Who was he? A cat caught stealing the cheese. I wasn't ready for him because I was in the moment of the scene of the play, with Kevin's eyes on me, and nothing else in the world, total immersion. We needed to stay there as long as we could, like catching a little hit of grass.

I took absolute control of the situation and pretended he wasn't there. I'm the director and I have to do that. Opening night is Saturday, June 26. I booked the theater until August 1, a five-week run, every night at eight o'clock, throughout the entire Bicentennial season. I don't like matinees. They seem unnatural. And no show on July Fourth, because no one is going to come to the theater on a night of revelry. I'm going to dance all day and I just don't want to be interrupted. I focused all my attention on Kevin. He was just out of high school and a little too sure of himself. But I need a challenge. Otherwise I can't be happy. Maybe he's left, I told myself, or he's sat down in the back row. Now show me what you got, Kevin. No. Let's get to work. Don't show me, just feel the storm. You're not showing anybody anything. Showing is pretending and this is the theater of the real thing. Dreams are real. That's another barrier we have to break.

But don't you see why it's so hard to be a good director? If I tell him what to do and he doesn't feel it then the scene will be dead and the play will be ruined. But I can't tell him that either! So I make myself as small as possible and let him take over the stage. He has a real presence, an internal fire and that's why I cast him for Armon. Armon is a seeker, but when he's asleep and dreaming he gives up control. What happens when the seeker is asleep? Let me see!

I stayed there as long as I could with a bubble around me to protect from the perplexed eyes of the man in the audience. They must be green eyes, perplexed and also forgiving.

The director can never hope because the hope will press in on the actor's consciousness. He will feel it in his hands, in his spine, and then he can't act. So I made myself small and gestured for Kevin to begin the scene. The moment Armon arrives in the village he searches for a place to sleep. He's exhausted from escaping the clutches of the people who promise him too much. He learns only at the last minute that their promises are a danger. The seeker goes in deep and sometimes has trouble climbing out. That's where we find him in this scene, climbing out, and he has a real physical dance with a farmer's daughter. The dance is his transference and now he's too tired to stand. But all his nerves are glowing!

Lie down, Armon, in the loft of the barn, and close your eyes. You don't see the storm coming, a storm that's real, we're going to make it rain on the stage, and just inside his head, the storm of uncertainty, self-doubt, and fear, and the juices of the storm will feed him, but he doesn't understand it yet. The storm, with all the elemental energy, is a nutrient and as the storm wracks him it gives him life. The sky is darkening, quietly, quietly, almost imperceptibly. The ends of your nerves are alive to it but not your consciousness. They are like the animals in the forest that sense an earthquake or a tornado. Humans could be this way, too, alive to everything around them. If only they could muster their glowing nerves. Be alive, Kevin, and also asleep. The dream isn't frightening at first. Drift away, rest, Armon, it's quiet and warm in the hayloft, you've saved your own life, you've done something profound!

Let yourself go, both Armon and Kevin, the two of you are merging before my eyes, one man becoming the other and the other becoming him. Stay there, because the audience has to merge in, too. Stay, stay, keep it another beat, and then, a wave. A wave pushes against that wave and another right behind it, the one in the back getting ahead of all the others, that's a storm. Everything goes out of order. The linear is fractured by the storm. Death comes before life, Armon, slowly, but violently, you will come to see.

Rest a while, Kevin, have some water. You're letting go, you feel the difference? I saw it with my own two eyes, the storm took you this time, and you didn't know to be conscious of fear, but it was terrifying! Drink some water. You want a beer? I think there's more from the other day. I'll get you a beer. You deserve it.

To get the beer I had to break the spell I'd cast and so I changed my mind. Let's wait for the beer. I want a beer, too, but I'm not ready. Drink your water, taste it on your lips, sit for a minute and then we'll do it again. I could feel the compassion, but also the confusion of those green eyes touching my shoulders and my hair from all the way across the theater, but I had to wait for it, I had to wait to soak in the green eyes.

Back up on the stage, Kevin! Do you feel the power in letting go? Remember, the storm comes slowly, a surprise, like the first day of earth, every time.

Between Kevin's second and third time the man moved closer to the stage. Did he wish to come all the way to the front, sit next to me in the second row, and then think better of it? Did he hesitate because he couldn't help himself? Sneaking up on me! He was looking down when I noticed him sitting in the middle of the house, writing in a notebook. Then he gazed out and his face was filled with astonishment.

I let Kevin go and go, seven, eight, nine times, and I went into a kind of trance. The tremors, the wind, shook through me. I dreamed a waking dream I was in France and smoke or fog came over the hillside, and machine gun fire that made everything around me shake. I, Sagittarius, was born of fire. Kevin was feeling the groove, Armon pulsing to life. Since I was his creator I pulsed, too, in time that was out of time.

When I said, Let's have that beer, I turned to walk up the center aisle and he was standing there. I gasped, as if he or I was naked. You turned that actor into a storm, he said. Yes. I discovered the storm inside him. His trouble is he's a little cool.

Paul Silk

"He's a little cool," she said. She was more solid and real than I had thought. She had weight. I couldn't believe this. I couldn't believe she wore shoes, tall boots, actually. I couldn't believe she had a hand to shake mine, a strong hand, actually. So strangely, I thought, a gunner's hand.

Charlene, Charlene, I—I had been watching her work for about an hour. She wanted something more from the actor. He was a little cocky, perhaps deliberately rejecting her direction. After a while she bore down on him.

"You're from the paper? Follow me," she said, "it's time for a break. They don't need me around for that." She had a deep laugh. She turned right outside the theater and we walked toward Pine Street. She lit a cigarette. "Do you?"

"No, never have."

"It's just a short walk."

"Where?"

"A little place I like. You'll have a drink with me in the afternoon?"

"No, I shouldn't," I said. "Who knows what it will do to me?"

"You talk that way I don't want to find out."

I looked ahead of me. The world was blank.

"Reporters don't drink anymore? Never met one who doesn't like to wet his lip."

I opened and closed my lips. Nothing came out.

"It's about the story, right?"

Charlene, I—.

"You know, you walk with your hands stuffed deep in your pockets."

Paul Silk

The walls of the dark room were covered with paintings. We took stools at one of the corners of the bar so that it would be easier to talk. She ordered two whiskeys and I took out my notebook.

"Put that away for now. On second thought..." She took the notebook and wrote:

Susan Painter
Dancer and theater director
4423 Osage Avenue
386-3312

Then she handed it back.

"My father drinks a lot of whiskey. Wild Turkey. It's kind of a family joke," I said.

"Oh yeah? What's he do, besides drink Wild Turkey?"

"I wish I could answer that. He owns a business. The family business."

"A mystery."

"Maybe it is or maybe it isn't."

"Your mother?"

"High school English teacher."

"No, spaceman. Does she think whatever your father does is mysterious?"

She was interviewing me. "I wish I could answer that."

She tapped the top of my head. "You live inside there." The whiskey became smooth on the third sip and we clinked glasses. The last time I had been in a bar in the middle of the day was on some lost corner of Kensington with my father. They called him "Doc."

Her hair was the color of honey. And amber light that shined down on the bar reflected the same color light. It was warm. I struggled to think of the right interview questions to ask.

Susan Painter

A painting hung on the wall opposite me. He couldn't see it but I could. It was an abstract painting with a long perspective, like the horizon. At the end, as if you were looking into a three-dimensional object, was a single point of green, just like his eyes. I distracted myself from the painting and from staring directly into his eyes, by asking him questions. His vague answers frustrated me, but if he gave me solid information I might get bored. His head seemed to float like a cloud above the bar.

The truth was I needed a break. The session with Kevin had drained me. I needed a different rhythm. The whiskey woke me up and I ordered another for me and for him. He didn't protest. You're deceptive, I said, just to see. Oh? I smiled and looked into my drink. You smile a lot, he said. No, he said, You seem to wear that smile. I like my teeth, I said. I like them too, he answered. See? I said. You're deceptive. You're supposed to be reporting a story. So what's that thing on your finger, Charlie? (In my family lore, my mother, a barmaid, had said the same thing to my father in the bar in Paris where she worked. He had married his high school girlfriend right before shipping off.) I'm sorry, I really don't need to know. (My mother said something a little different.) He cleared his throat in the sweetest, most despairing way. His eyes landed somewhere, far from the corner of 13th and Pine. Freedom, he said, with pen in hand, seems like a tormented affair.

15.

The Ring and the Gilded Cage

Jeanette Johnson

Working in Dr. Fishman's office is a piece of cake. The hardest thing is remembering the terms of all the dental procedures and acting like you know what they mean. You never say, "You're here to have your tooth pulled, Mrs. Sylvester?" No, it's "extraction." These are the words I try to use when talking with a patient: composite (Dr. Fishman is proud to use this new procedure to fix a chipped tooth), Novocain (you have to say this word with a smile), molar and incisor, amalgam, and impression. We have drawers filled with these impressions, which look like they come from skeletons. But I like to look at them. Sometimes I think they might start clacking like it was Halloween. Dr. Fishman makes crowns and bridges, which is kind of funny, but most people come in to have their teeth cleaned. At least a filling is a filling. Dr. Fishman is a stickler for check-ups and so we have to make sure each patient is scheduled when she leaves. Check-ups are the best way to find out if someone has a cavity or if their gums are bleeding. "Do you still want to go to school for hygiene?" he asked me last Thursday. He caught me looking through the drawers of impressions. The Doctor writes the patient's name on it in magic marker. "Yes, Doctor," I answered. "Do you think I'm ready?" I didn't want to assume. "Maybe I still need to learn more." Dr. Fishman said that in three months I could start taking classes. He looked at me for a minute like he was thinking about something

133

and then he said, "After the Bicentennial."

I still have time to walk around Center City, even to wander a little and get "lost," because Dr. Fishman gives us an hour for lunch. I usually take lunch break early because he doesn't want the assistants and the hygienists to stop so soon. I go first, at 11:45. First I walk around and lately I've made a game of it looking for more Bicentennial banners, flags, and signs in the windows. "Oh, look at that one, they're advertising special Bicentennial handbags with red and white and blue leather, and Bicentennial boots!" I walk and I talk and I sing. Dr. Fishman says he knows the guy who designed the official Bicentennial emblem, with the Liberty Bell and "76." He's a patient. "Someday you'll meet him."

Dr. Fishman has been wearing white pants since the weather started to get warm. But I think he's excited for the Bicentennial. It's hard not to be. They say millions of people are going to come and they're going to see our great city. Today, I saw workers painting park benches red, white, and blue.

And that makes me laugh because downtown we're wearing red, white, and blue sequin dresses that the boss had made special for us to wear this spring and summer. He calls me "the African Princess." "You wear red, always red," he says. He has the thickest eyebrows to go along with the elephant ears. "This way you're always first, right? Red, white, and blue. Red is always first." He said this when the other girls couldn't hear. But I think he talks this way to all of us. Learning how to belly dance has been much harder than learning to be the receptionist in Dr. Fishman's office. My muscles ached for two weeks! "You turn yourself into a rubber band," the boss said, "and once you're a rubber band, you're a belly dancer. I couldn't be a belly dancer, but you can—and you will!" So I did. I can wiggle and jiggle like a rubber band now. Not only can I do it, but I love to do it, even when I'm not on the stage up on the second floor. I want to wiggle and jiggle. I wiggle and jiggle in Dr. Fishman's office. No one can see me doing it and no one knows. Mama and Daddy and Granny don't know either. I leave my dress at the boss's place downtown and I remove my makeup before I come home.

The boss has big plans for the Bicentennial and I'm worried I'm going to have to tell my parents. I secretly wish Granny could see me! Shows every night at eight and ten starting in June and going to August. "People from all over the world," the boss says. He's from Lebanon and some of the dancers are too. One is from Iran and another is from Spain. She's a flamenco dancer normally. She showed me the other day while we were getting ready. She taught me to clap the right way, using my palms. That's what I like about the boss's place. Everybody is from somewhere else. It's so different from Overbrook. Being around all these people from all over the world made me think of my sister Charlene and her jewelry, especially the turquoise ring Paul bought her after they moved to Denver. If I had that ring I would think of her. It would be like she was with me, all the time, even if I only wear it only on special occasions, like after the show when the boss brings us drinks and I listen and don't say a thing, everybody speaking in their different accents, and me from 63rd and Lebanon wondering how I got there. I'm always amazed at myself. Even in Dr. Fishman's office, saying, "We're going to schedule your crown for next Friday." I'll wear the ring when I'm finished dancing. "Look at that ring, where did you get it?" And me, "It's a Navajo ring, from Arizona. It was my sister's." No one downtown knows about my sister.

Granny told me Paul was working at the paper. I could still remember Charlene's number, so I dialed it and some gruff-sounding white man answered. I almost hung up. I was at a pay phone at the corner of 19th and JFK. The buses were so noisy! "Hello, sir, can you connect me with Paul Silk?"

"Who?"

"His name is Paul. He has curly hair."

"Silk? He doesn't work here anymore."

For a minute I thought, Oh, no, Paul's already lost the job, something terrible must have happened. And then I realized the guy on the phone didn't know that he got rehired. I almost mentioned my sister, since that guy had her line, but I didn't. I'm glad I didn't. I don't like talking about her.

"I think he works there again," I said and he said, "Let me see."

He put the phone down but didn't put me on hold so I could hear him asking someone else if they knew if Paul Silk was in the newsroom. And then that person asked someone else. I could hear all of it. Finally, "I'm going to transfer you, lady," and he hit the button before I could even say thanks.

When I heard Paul's voice I got a terrible pang in my stomach. I think I was nervous anyway, but his voice reminded me of my sister. My stomach was wiggling and jiggling but on the inside and I felt a little sick.

"The incredible wonderful delicious Jeanette?"

"I'm not a ham sandwich, Paul."

"You're better than a ham sandwich, much better. More like a chicken salad sandwich."

I laughed because it was so stupid. "I saw you getting off the El."

"What, you did? When?"

"Two-and-a-half months ago. That's how I knew you were back. No one tells me anything."

"I like to keep it mysterious."

"Me, too!" I said even though it wasn't really true. I wanted to learn to be mysterious. Everyone knows I can't keep a secret.

"It's so great to hear your voice," he said, and I could tell he was almost starting to get choked up.

"It's hard, maybe."

"No, it's wonderful! You sound like a real grown woman."

"I am!"

"I mean really like you own the world. Jeanette! My long lost sister."

I'd forgotten he liked to call me his sister. It was true, but not true also. "Your sister has gotten old, Paul. She's almost on her own."

"Not like me. I'm like thirteen again, living in my parent's house. My mother makes my breakfast in the morning."

"She does?"

"No, she doesn't! But there's always hope for Mrs. Silk."

"Oh Paul, she's a good mom. Just don't cross her."

"Never."

"Can I ask you a question?"

"Depends! No, of course. And when can we have lunch or something so I can see you and not just hear your tasty voice?"

"I get an hour every day for lunch."

"Then next week some time."

"Paul, I want to ask you. You remember that ring?"

"Ring?" He didn't answer right away and at first I thought well, this is Paul and he always takes a long time to answer. But this was taking a while and I was at a pay phone.

"Paul?"

"The ring?"

"The ring, Paul, you bought for Charlene in Arizona, with the turquoise stone. Do you still have it? I mean, you have it, don't you?" Then I thought, Maybe he just couldn't keep it. But why didn't he offer it to me? He must have sold it. That's why he can't answer. He doesn't want to admit it. "Paul?"

"The ring? I think I have it somewhere. In one of my bags… still packed."

"Can you find it, do you think?"

"I can look."

"Paul, you'll tell me if you don't want to."

"No, I want to. I want to—I mean, of course, Jeanette, the greatest Jeanette. You should have the ring. I promise. I'll find it and call you."

"I'll call you in a week. Give me your desk line direct." I forgot to thank him before I hung up, but I couldn't stay on any longer.

Paul Silk

The sun had put itself in perfect dalliance with City Hall tower, just enough to the east at this hour of late morning that it descended gently to my feet as I turned to walk down Broad Street. The air was warm and calm and the breeze ticklish. Someone was even sweeping the sidewalk. I had an hour and fifteen minutes until the lunch with Jeanette, which was to be at a place she recommended, the Gilded Cage. I passed one turn-of-the century office tower after the other, stolid, upright, handsome piles with their jaunty optimistic decorative scrolls and carvings of ships and crests and bells, and yes, gold-leaf engravings: gilded cages, tarnished, rusted, sometime slathered and blackened. And yet even with the sun and mountains, Denver had never given me this impression, of holding a life, or lives or stories.

I crossed under the archway at City Hall, under the elephant eyes and hippo noses carved into the stone, and into the courtyard. "Do you know what just happened up there, on the fourth floor?" someone said. She had her hand on my arm, in the other hand a clipboard, and a "Recall Rizzo" button on the lapel of her jacket. She was no older than twenty-five.

"I do know," I said.

"Then you know City Council just passed Frank Rizzo's tax increase? Property tax up nearly thirty percent, wage tax—"

"Don't worry, ma'am, I'm with the paper. I think my colleagues are on their way to try to get Mr. Rizzo on the record. I'd like to sign your petition, but my profession forbids it. My own dear grandmother is out here collecting signatures, too. Her name is Simone, maybe you've run across her."

"Every signature counts," she said. "It's our future." Just then I noticed a baby stroller a couple of feet away.

"Well, the Mayor is doing a good job promoting your cause. Every word out of his mouth—You're up to how many now?"

"We were told over 120,000."

"I wish you both luck," I responded and tried to step away.

"Oh, yes, it's all for him and this one." She meant she had another on the way. "If we don't fix this place no one will."

"1976, it has a good ring to it. This could be the year." Beyond the woman there were a dozen others, clipboards in hand.

"But Mr. Reporter, do you think we'll make it? You know more than I do he lied to get reelected. He lied! And now we're to pay for his corruption and incompetence. And what he did to your paper, sir! I don't know how you can be so calm."

"It's our duty."

"We are ordinary people and we're fed up!"

Now I understood: the people were already celebrating the Bicentennial. This was it. I took the woman's name and her phone number. I only had to convince Stan Woszek, the editor, I had an angle. I passed through the south arch, past the popcorn man, eyes dancing, across the sharp angle of the sun. The Union League was already festooned with bunting. I turned onto Walnut Street and already, an hour before lunch, the sidewalk was crowded, on the north side of the street especially, where the sun dangled, and reflecting off the storefront windows glimmering patterns and designs on the sidewalk. What did Bellis say, in his poem? *The same swell, pulse, and morning/ the steam shoots through pipes/a jet fish eludes the shark. Above the line you recognize/there is no line. Below the line you recognize/only distant mind.* After a while I sat down on a bench in Rittenhouse Square and looked up. Above the line? The sun was still there.

"The sheep used to graze here, did you know," the scrawny old man next to me on the bench proclaimed.

"Maybe so!" I replied, not anxious to hear more, content in my mind's reverie, the first I'd felt this alive since coming home.

"No, really, they did, but they've been run off by these foxes," he said, pleased with his joke, gesturing to some attractive women on a bench across the way, and others sitting on the fountain's edge, the stone wall, passing by in tall leather boots, black girls and white girls.

"I thought this was where they did the public executions."

"You mean of dirty old men like me?"

"Dirty young ones, too."

"No, that was Logan Square, my friend. I'm sure of it." He was a serious historian now.

For a moment, I recalled Charlene and I here in the square. She allowed us—she said it was OK for us to come here, to hold hands. Holding hands, sitting on that bench over there, or that one, or standing by the lion, sharing a cigarette. I would invent our dreams and she would take notes on a story she was working on. Was all this here now, still here, trapped in the gilded cage?

"If only we could stay here, in Rittenhouse Square, all the time, forever, baby," she'd said, glancing up from her notebook and continuing making notes even before she finished the sentence. She was made of iron, I thought then.

"There's one over there," the old man elbowed me. Did he have a brogue, as if from a far crevice?

"What's that?"

"A red fox, my friend," he said, and nodded toward the grass field along 18th Street. I tried not to laugh. My companion was incorrigible. "Look!" he said, and elbowed me. I gazed hesitantly in that direction. I didn't want to look. Or I couldn't allow myself to. "You see her, don't you? The one dancing, if that is dancing? Wake up, my boy, quit your dreaming!"

What was it? He elbowed me a second time. I was somehow captive. He pointed. A woman, in fact, was dancing, in short, explosive bursts, between the trees, as if she wanted to communicate in some new, raw language.

Her long, honey-colored hair flowed as she whipped across the park. The red fox was Susan. She was working out her Bicentennial dance.

"Look at her gallop and pounce."

"What?"

"Legs as long as Lehigh Avenue."

His face was splotched, red continents across the drawn cheeks.

"Now why is she out here dancing? She could be inside, you know."

"Why not?

"Because she wants your eyes on her, the lass. She's an exhibitionist."

I gazed up at the sky.

"You see! You can't take your eyes away."

Should I go over? No I couldn't disturb her. I'd better not interrupt. The old man got up. "I'm off for church," he said, by which he must have meant it was time for a shot and a beer.

I still had half an hour until it was time to meet Jeanette.

Jeanette Johnson

I was already sitting in the window of the Gilded Cage secretly wiggling and jiggling when Paul came in. I'd ordered a chicken salad sandwich on a French croissant because I like the way it tastes with green grapes cut in half and because I wanted to pay for my own lunch. I didn't want Paul to think he had to pay for me. At the Gilded Cage you order at the counter. Paul came in, sat down, and just started talking like nothing in the world had ever happened between the last time I saw him (not counting my sister's funeral) and today. "I'm feeling Russian today," he said, and I looked at him funny, "a little tragic." Then he changed his mind, "No, maybe not Russian, maybe German," as if I had any idea what he was saying. "Germans like sunshine because it's healthy." Then he stopped himself, maybe because he thought I might be offended when he said the word healthy because it isn't fair that my sister got sick and died.

I wanted to tell him to go over to the counter to order but he got going again about being Russian or German. I must have said "uh-huh" a thousand times nodding and almost cracking up. What he was trying to explain to me is that some Jewish people are German and some are Russian. That's where they came from. Some like him are both. He gave me examples of the two sides of his family, the Felds and Birnbaums on his mom's side are from Germany and the Gordons and the Silks on his dad's side are from Russia. "I'm half-and-half," he said, "split right down the middle." He said all the Jews originally came from the same place but after they were kicked out of Spain they ended up in separate places and took on the traits of the people who already lived there. So German Jews are "austere," "practical," "judgmental," and "waspy."

"What you mean waspy? Got stingers?" I asked. I know people like that. (Paul's mother, Mrs. Silk, taught me to always ask when I wasn't sure of a word.)

Paul wiggled his eyebrows funny and said that wasp means "White Anglo-Saxon Protestant."

"You mean white regular people who aren't Jewish?"

"Or Catholic or poor or anything but people who talk like this"— he pinched his nose and kept talking—"or wear seersucker suits."

"German Jews are like that?"

He said, "You ever met my grandmother Simone?"

"And Russians?" I asked because now, I had to know.

"Dreamy, impractical, tragic, always shooting themselves in the foot."

"So which one likes sunshine?"

He thought about this awhile. "Germans like sunshine because it makes them feel healthy. It increases their vitamin D"—was he making this up?—"and because they know it won't last. The Russian Jew thinks it will be good for business."

I started to laugh. And he laughed and then he got serious. "Here we go. The issue of justice, or injustice. The German Jew expects there to be justice. He thinks it's possible! The Russian believes injustice is proof that God is laughing at him."

I didn't understand this either but it didn't matter because the lady brought over my chicken salad sandwich. Paul told her he wanted the same thing but she said he had to come up to the counter and pay for it first. That's the way they do it here. Finally, I knew something Paul didn't.

When he came back I told him about Dr. Fishman. "Is he a German or a Russian Jew," he asked. "German? Everything has to be a certain way," I said. But I wasn't sure. I was a little confused. Then I told him about the Lebanese place, about how I can wiggle and jiggle, and about the boss with the elephant's ears. I hadn't told anyone, not even Trish. "You can't tell anyone in my family or yours!" "Yes, ma'am," he said, and then he asked if he could come see me perform some time. Why not? "Will you?" "Yes, I want to. Can I bring a friend?" he asked. But before I had a chance to answer he took the turquoise ring out of his pocket, reached out for my hand, and slipped it on my finger.

16.

Paul Tracks Down a Lead

Paul Silk

I wanted to touch her honey-colored hair. Not just touch it, but smell it. Not just smell it but let it engulf me.

Did I have this wave of need with Charlene? She smells—smelled— of warm herbs, like the earth itself. I became addicted to that smell. The smell of all time before or since.

Was this somehow different? Everything with Charlene was ordered, put in place, in sequence. One thing led to another. Not as in a dream but as if preordained and therefore eternal. She never struggled with a decision. She never wavered once it was made. The cancer came after her, opened a hole inside her, emptied her out, filled the hole with pain.

"It's gnawing at me," she had said. I tried to turn my hand into a balm, but the pain was too thick already. Her skin was still beautiful, even then.

"You won't ever betray me," she said. We were sitting in her front room. Her mother was playing piano.

"I could never."

Susan Painter

He came to me at the theater on Friday afternoon with news. I wasn't allowed to tell anyone until Sunday. I can't understand why

143

they decided to hold onto the story for two days, but Paul said the Sunday paper mattered most. Here it is: in an interview that was supposed to be about the tax hike and the recall Rizzo had told the reporters that a bunch of radicals were planning an assault during the Bicentennial. Who are these radicals? Rizzo didn't give any details. Did the reporters ask? I don't know if they asked but we're doing an investigation ourselves, he said. Because I don't believe it, I said. He's calling in federal troops. Soldiers? Fifteen-thousand soldiers, that's what I wanted to tell you. The Bicentennial. Terrorists are coming? He's making it up. Show me proof. No one has proof, not yet. I only wanted you to know. He's capable of anything. I'm reporting on the recall. I have an angle, he said. I kissed him. The recall is heating up. Susan, he said, do you see? The recall is a celebration of the Bicentennial. That's your angle? That's my angle. I kissed him again, his lips soft, supple. Have you signed? Of course, I said, and that's what the troops are for. To stop the recall. I don't know if he can, he said. You can't be naïve, Paul, Frank Rizzo is a thug. But what about *Freedom*? Ticket sales? What about your dance? Can you dance with soldiers? I lit a cigarette. He doesn't get it, how an artist thinks. But that's OK, he doesn't groove that way. I don't care if I'm the only one out there. I'm dancing. Freedom has nothing to do with Frank Rizzo. It's up here. If you're emancipated. I beg to differ, he said, his eyes intent, wishing to speak. Tell me, Paul. I'm listening. Consider the tyrant. Rizzo is one. He might choose to restrict your freedom. Of course. I wanted to say I'd meant something different, but I kept silent. But that's not even what I want to imply, Susan, because I know you know that. It's the matter of the mind, Rizzo's tyranny. The lies, the arrests, the arbitrary decisions. You can't free your mind from it—certain people can't, I mean. The torture and the confusion are too great. Certain people get trapped in it. They can't free their minds. You're talking about someone you know, I said, but he didn't want to say more. I put out my cigarette and came closer. But of course you will dance, Susan, he said, finally, and I let the sweet sadness linger in the air.

17.

Sam Feels The Walls Closing In

Sam Silk

Paul put the meatloaf in the oven. His mother was at a meeting. He knows his way around the kitchen. That was the arrangement he had with Charlene. They both worked late but he took care of the house. She really had everything just as she wanted it. And my son acquiesced. Now he needed to know what did I want to drink? What kind of salad dressing did I prefer? Did I want ketchup with the meatloaf? No, I didn't want ketchup with the meatloaf. Do we have any Tabasco? I had enough on my mind not to be pestered. I should have looked forward to a meal with him, alone, but how could I? Payments had to be made.

He was covering the recall drive. He said it was a living symbol of the Bicentennial. If that's the case it will fail, I said, and he said the campaign could win even if the recall fails. Thousands of people, many who have never participated before, have decided to save the city. What's with all the business about leftists? Is there proof? Too soon to tell, he said. But today the campaign announced it had enough signatures to get the recall on the ballot, two weeks before the deadline. The heat is on. These political movements rarely pan out, I said. I got up and made a drink and brought it back to the table.

Then he stirred a little and fixed his eyes on me. What was coming? Then: Words stumbled out, slow as usual, but confused. Finally I understood, he'd seen Silk sweaters for sale. Somewhere over here on

Lancaster Avenue and somewhere in Kensington. I shrugged. We sell everywhere and what of it? You think it's a problem? He started again, first with Lancaster Avenue and then 5th Street. A toy store and a variety store. He fixated on that. He couldn't get over it. They weren't clothing stores. Worse in his mind, the owners of the stores seemed afraid to discuss it, the sweaters some kind of bugaboo. Bugaboo is the word he used. I went over to the bar just to get some space. The table started to feel claustrophobic. This modern, open plan house. I couldn't breathe. I poured myself a drop more and got my footing. I couldn't sit down.

There wasn't any way to explain it. Because I didn't know exactly what went on. But that racket was going to make the payment to the bank, that's all. And tomorrow I could decide. Tomorrow and tomorrow and tomorrow. By the end of it we'll have our feet on the ground. A good manager, a good creative businessman will come along and I'll put him in charge. Someone who sees the value.

I ceded no ground to Paul. I have no reason for shame. You want to feel shame, go ahead. I told him, go find more stores. They're out there. All over the city, you'll discover. And expanding. These are good sweaters at a solid value. They last! The Silk Line is the mark of distinction. When were these made? Those sweaters aren't the latest line. Did Paul understand that? I'd have to explain the business. That could take time. He sat on the ottoman with his sleeves rolled up and his hands on his knees. Your mother doesn't understand it either. It's complicated and I don't have time to explain it to her late at night. There is no time. I saw myself and I saw him and I couldn't make sense of it. What I wanted to say or what he needed me to say. Could he perceive it? I was calm, now sitting. We were both sitting. Denver might have been closer. Damn it to hell. I'm not going to be the one to lose the mill. He was silent, now. Nothing more? No. I sensed pity. I couldn't take pity. Stuff your pity! Wasn't pity. I decided it was affection, calm, loving, a kind of embrace. I had to accept it. Then he spoke, in the same earnest way he would as a teenager. I memorized what he said and I felt our roles reversing: First of all, I don't believe you, he said. I can't even understand you. Do you know that?

It seems like I left and everything became inscrutable and somehow perverse. Charlene wanted light, that's what she wanted because here no light would do, not even at the newspaper. We could never get to the bottom of it. You see, Dad? Now I'm the one who feels afraid. I don't want to know. I'm afraid to know.

Then he paused and I waited. I met his gaze and then I let it go. He asked me this: And Monte? Is he wrapped up in this? Is he?

I lied to him and said no.

Paul Silk

Right there in his chair he seemed to shrink. The man became smaller and smaller right before my eyes.

18.

Monte Reflects on Darkness and Light

Louis Turner

"Listen to Louis," I say to Eddie. "It's time." He doesn't give me a look or say anything. No response. I can't tell if he's even thinking. "I never stop thinking," I say to myself.

"I'm not clear yet," he says.

It's Friday. The boss is at lunch up on the corner. It's time. "You know what I was thinking? Let's say you're the boss. You can't go to that joint."

"What joint?"

"The joint up on the corner where he goes."

"I don't need to go to that joint. You don't need to. Monte don't need to."

"I got you thinking," I say.

I'm tossing keys in my hand. The key to the delivery van, the shop floor, the warehouse, the storeroom, everything but the main office. I hate not being sly. The point is it's time for the boss to understand. The percentages. "What percent we say?"

"Why you think it's time for that?"

"Give me that number, come on man." Sometimes I have to get real. "We need a radio in this joint." No, a hi-fi system.

"Thirty on top."

149

"Thirty on top of the arrangements because we're the ones who make it. And Krishna?"

"Why you need to know every detail?"

"You tell him right now when he comes in. 'Boss, we're putting everything in tip-top shape.' Say it, 'The knitter third from the front on the left side near the window our man Krishna got it running.' He'll understand."

"Monte."

"You got to soften him up," I say.

"And when he shrugs? Man, it ain't that simple. You read too many comic books."

"I read and I think."

"Let me do the thinking, Louis!"

"When he shrugs you make it plain. You go in all alone. It's Friday, everything's cool. Man, the birds in the courtyard are singing, the stray cat's meowing, and he's had two drinks. Make your voice real soft, real smooth. Nothing creaky. And you say it's gonna be thirty on top. Then he'll mumble, 'I like the arrangement the way it is, Eddie. I don't think there's any reason to change it.' Then you hum and haw a while—"

"Why am I stalling? I don't need to stall. He's the one has to stall."

Louis is real smart. "He's stalling. It's Friday and this morning you practically handed him a wad of cash. He's not expecting this. He's not soft enough. You got to turn him into mud."

"We don't want trouble."

"We want it easy, Eddie, you damn well know it. But he's only mud."

"Man, what?"

"So then you bring out the latest picture Krishna made. The fall design. It says, right on there, 'The Silk Line,' just like in the old days. Krishna found that somewhere. Now he's coming soft. You got to use your head!" Eddie never thinks of things this way. There's dark and there's light, good and evil. A superhero is both. Krishna is both. You got to know how to use the gods. They can give and they can remove. "Then you say, 'But the arrangement's going to change. Otherwise.' And stop there. Don't keep talking, Eddie. Don't talk right over yourself. Then Krishna walks in, scares the life out of that fool."

Monte Johnson

Sometimes he's good and sometimes he's bad, sometimes he doesn't know the difference. But *shouldn't* he know? He was a straight-A student! His daddy taught him and his mama—his mama goes to church when she isn't tired. His granny's been around the block. She sees right through everything!

Fuck, fuck, fuck.

What if the day was divided into light and dark? Oh yeah, right. That's called night and day. I mean the day. Light and dark. And the night? Dark and darker? When you sign your draft papers they should say, "Welcome to the United States military. Be prepared to kill and see the sun rise every day." No, I haven't been staying out that late. I have to shower and go to work. (The sun rises when I'm in the shower. I don't see it.)

The day is divided into dark and light.

I don't have anything against Sam Silk. Or Harriett, his wife, Mrs. Silk. Or their son, Paul. I love him like a brother.

Sam Silk pays me money. He is afraid of me. I haunt him in the light and in the dark.

19.

What To Do About Monte?

Charles Johnson

I'm trying to get something out of Monte. I mean, give me a sniff of whatever it is you're smoking. Yes sir, he says. He used to give me that fake military stuff long before he went off to Vietnam. Now it's extra nasty. What do they do over there at Silk Industries? Print money?

Working looms? Oiling the machines? Sweeping the floor? Back in the day a Negro could sweep the floor. Period. Don't forget to shovel the coal ash. He couldn't even deliver the coal. You been there two months and what now, I hear you saved Grandma. They give you a raise for that? You get this, I'm still the one talking and you looking at the floor.

Deliveries? That it? Following in your daddy's footsteps! You're going store-to-store delivering sweaters. Oh yeah? You ever come into my territory? It's not like that? That so? Tell you what, I'm sure it's not the same because I've been doing it for fifteen years. Men's, women's, kid's. OK, lightweight for spring? That's it, sweaters? You're not sure. You're not sure. I'll give Sam a call, check in. Now you shrug, Monte. What's that? He doesn't want to know? You got it all tangled up, kid, one of Monte's riddles. Let's see if Granny can figure it out.

Elsa Franklin Smith

Charles is making himself sicker and sicker over Monte, though he did what he wanted him to do, got off the street and into a job. I know how it is with men, even men like Charles, they have to be the man. Something about Jewish men is different. Their mothers make them passive and their fathers give all the power to their sisters. The sisters want to be the ones in charge. Charles has too much pride and that's a dangerous thing for a black man. I don't know about Monte. Last few years he cut off his pride. He did it on purpose. He wanted us to think it was drugs. If Monte's on drugs there wasn't anything to be done and that's what he wanted us to think, he's too far gone. It wasn't drugs he was doing in that boarded up house. I gather he was doing something else that put a little cash in his pocket. Something worse, Elsa, is that what you think? Selling himself. But I can't say it out loud.

Now I see those two gentlemen pick him up every day. They think I'm still sleeping, but an old lady like me doesn't need much sleep. Monte takes a shower and gets out when his sister yells in there like the world is ending. He takes his time to look good. Now, who's he trying to impress? He thinks we haven't noticed.

He doesn't look like he's going in to do factory work. Back in my day a fellow dressed like that if he owned a shop, as my husband did, a barber's shop, or a nightclub. The ones who could get factory work were filthy all the time. Domestics dressed decently, but only because they were required to. It wasn't exactly a matter of status. Monte dresses real well and then he leaves out. But those same two gentlemen don't bring him home. I'm not certain who does. Some nights he comes home real late, long past midnight, or later, into the morning, but I can't tell who drops him off.

It was on Sunday, in the evening, that Charles got to ask the boy some questions. Anita and I had just gone out for groceries and Jeanette was asleep. Just the two men in the house. Could have been the trouble. But Charles said he let the frustration get the best of him. He didn't believe Monte. "Can't be the truth." What can Granny find out? That's what he wanted to know. I said maybe he should call Sam Silk, but he said, "No, no, only Granny can find out the truth."

So I waited in the kitchen until the house was dark and eventually that boy came down. Someone had opened the window but now a chill came through.

"Shut it for me, Monte." He did what I asked, didn't say a word. "Aren't you cold in bare feet?"

"No, Granny."

"You want some sweet tea?"

"No, ma'am."

"A drink of water? That what you came for?"

"It's all right."

"But you came for something, Sonny."

"To see you, Granny."

"You think I was born yesterday?"

"I knew you were down here."

"Your daddy's hurting," I said.

"He'll be all right."

"Like he's lost hold." Did he get it?

"Supposed to be my problem?"

"You could give him a little, won't hurt." I went over to him by the sink, told him to move out of the way. I got out two glasses and ran us both some water. "Get me the lemon," I said.

I sat myself down and watched him standing there, leaning against the counter, swallowing like he had all the time in the world. His Adam's apple bobbing gently, as if it was lost in the ocean.

"Tell me where you go at night. That Cadillac brings you home, but where you been?"

"Granny has eyes all over her head!"

"Hush now. Sit down. It's all right. You like whoever you like. Your daddy don't care. Your mama don't care. Jeanette don't care. Granny don't care, Monte, but what's inside there? What are you looking for?"

"Here for interrogation, Sargent Granny!"

"No, Monte. You're a man. You fill this room as a man, not a boy. You go to work for Sam Silk!" Now look at me, Monte, I said to myself, look at me. If only he could see. "What do you go looking for?"

He tried to get up and I put my hand on his. "Stop fooling."

"Daddy can't take it," he mumbled.

"What, Sonny?"

Then he started up, all a jumble, too jumbled to follow exactly.

Something about the noise of Saigon. "The guns?" I said.

"No, no guns. Music mixed up with people talking and heat, the hot air, and the bloods and the geishas trying to get over. Forget it. Forget it, Granny."

"Go on, Sonny."

"That's it. Didn't you ask what I'm looking for? That's it. Takes me back there."

"And?"

"It takes me back there. That's it."

20.

Dr. Death Appears

Albert Birnbaum

My secretary, Patricia, patched through the call from my brother-in-law and client Sam Silk. It isn't unusual for Sam to call, but it isn't a common occurrence. In my line of work there are two types of clients. The first type needs to be sure his affairs are always in order. Our relationship is one of director (the client) and directed (the attorney). He will call and let me know how he wants to handle something and he'll want regular updates on the progress and the outcomes of the measures taken, either legal or financial or statutory. The second kind of client wishes for contact with the attorney only when an acute situation demands it and otherwise assumes his affairs are in order. In this case, the relationship is between the counseled (the client) and the counselor (the attorney). Aside from the obvious complicating factors of our family relationship, Sam is this exact kind of second client *ipso facto*. The complicating factor is a serious one and it means the responsibility for keeping Silk Industries legally above board and financially above water is mine, assuming I have been granted access to all the information. In any case, Sam doesn't call often and when he does I clear my mind of other distractions.

I have previously mentioned my client's paramount desires for personal privacy and for survival. By that second term he means he wishes to make sure the company, which was handed down to him by his father, Abe, and which has produced the significant wealth that allows the family to live in comfort, endure as long as possible as a productive manufacturer. Perhaps his great weakness is that he can't bear to be the one to lose it. (In this sense the astute observer will conclude that Sam has been the first type of client, who has directed me to help him find the legal and financial means to survive and I have abided that role, even at times when it has made me uncomfortable.)

It was Friday mid-afternoon when he called. I put Sam on hold and got up to close my office door. Right away I could anticipate that something was wrong. Even the phone line carried a different sound, tinnier than usual. I was correct on that account. Sam was calling from a pay phone on the corner of Front and Jasper Streets, a few blocks from the mill. Is there a fire? These kinds of fires have become all too common in that section of the city. I even entertained, if only for a split second, that Sam had set the fire deliberately as a way out of his company's difficult financial predicament. Front and Jasper, where Sam was standing when he called, is right underneath the tracks of the El. The first thing I asked is whether he was safe, standing there. He didn't respond. I asked him why he hadn't called from his office. Again, he didn't respond. The El passed overhead and I couldn't hear a thing. I thought I lost him. Then his voice came through hesitantly. He seemed confused. Had he gone too heavy on the Wild Turkey during lunch? "Things have gotten a little out of control," he said. I had no reason not to believe him, but I needed facts. I had no information beyond what I already knew about some of the business practices and some of his employees. I sensed he didn't feel safe returning to his office at the mill. He thanked me. He was breathing heavily. I insisted he get on the El and get out of the neighborhood. From there he could take a taxi home. "I think I've done a terrible thing," he said and I advised him to come see me in the morning at my apartment. "I'll supply the bagels and the coffee," I told him.

Albert Birnbaum

Sam rang the doorbell of my apartment on the sixteenth floor of the Rittenhouse Claridge promptly at 9:30 a.m. on Saturday. He was wearing a windbreaker unzipped, a bright green alligator shirt, loafers without socks, and was cleanly shaven. I mention these details because they indicate a level of wellbeing. But even established facts can be deceiving.

I poured the coffee from my new Mr. Coffee and set out a plate with four bagels next to an open foil of cream cheese and a bottle of milk for the coffee. I offered him some Sweet'N Low because I know he likes it sugared. He commented on the view over the square and we talked about the Bicentennial and the promising start for the Phillies. Without me asking he started to talk about Silk Industries, an ongoing issue with his employees, and his worry about one of them in particular, Monte Johnson. He asked if I would listen and just let him talk, which I agreed to, and encouraged. It was obvious he needed to get this off his chest. I advised him that he allow me to take notes while he spoke and after hemming and hawing quite a bit, he agreed. His concern, he stated right away, was that neither Harriett nor Paul find out, at least not right now, what he was going to tell me. He didn't mention Alan. I nodded agreement.

Before he started I asked him to be fully forthcoming. I told him there was nothing to be gained by hiding things from me. But I wasn't sure if this warning was heeded.

He began and began again, each time starting over and pushing back into history so that I would understand. So that I would understand and forgive? Quite possibly. Five years ago a crime wave hit Kensington as a result of poverty, an influx of poor and destitute Puerto Ricans with low education and limited work potential into the neighboring Norris Square, the mafia's flooding the city with cocaine, and a nearly fatal and final collapse in the manufacturing economy of Kensington. Sam identified these factors specifically. For a small businessman he is remarkably open-minded and sensitive to the bigger picture. This may be my sister Harriett's influence.

Silk Industries became an easy target. Like other still-operating family-owned firms, there were few security measures in place. The mill was burglarized several times and Sam was held up at gunpoint. Sam was determined to keep the business operating. He hired a man by the name of Eddie Williams to protect him, his employees (only seventeen of them by 1971), and the property. Eddie had been a bodyguard for a state senator but he, himself, had a criminal record going back to 1955, when he was fourteen. About a year later, as the crime wave continued, Eddie Williams hired his older brother's old grade school classmate, Louis Turner. Both men are Negro. By 1972, half of Sam's employees were black, an unusual practice in Kensington that was met with different kinds of threats Eddie and Louis were able to repel. Once, in January 1974, when Sam and Harriett were in Denver while Charlene was undergoing one of the unsuccessful treatments for cancer of the pancreas, a group of white men, aged fifteen to sixty-four, tried to set the mill on fire. Louis caught them and drove them away. Louis has a maniacal nature that might scare Attila the Hun.

Sam thinks this success emboldened Eddie and Louis. In April of that year they began extorting Sam with threats of injury and violence. Were they members of the Black Mafia? I interrupted Sam to ask the question. He said they weren't, as far as he knew.

"Just a couple guys trying to get over," he told me. Instead of informing me about the extortion, or going to the police, he went along with it. In essence, he wanted to help them.

Why not do it legally? Make a new entity? I jotted these questions down on my pad.

As I understand it, the initial scheme was this: Eddie and Louis were confident that they could convince small retailers to stock the sweaters made by Silk Industries. Sam had become reliant on railroads, utilities, and parochial schools, which purchased his customized sweaters direct and made to order. (With some connections to party leaders, politicians, and bureaucrats I have been able to help Sam keep those contracts renewing.) Eddie and Louis said that there were dozens of small clothing stores, some of them neighborhood institutions, all throughout the black neighborhoods of Philadelphia. Some of those shopkeepers were black, others white, others were Jewish. Some even were Chinese or Korean. They would sell remnants from old lines of sweaters to those stores, this unofficial business would be off the books, and they would split the profit with Sam.

Some of the cash from this venture was being used to pay off one of the bank loans that I had secured for the mill in 1971. The other loan was about to come due, which I reminded him then.

He nodded and fumbled with his bagel, hands shaking. I handed him a napkin. I offered a second cup of coffee. He went back to his narrative. The scheme seemed to work. Sam was able to sell off old inventory at almost no cost and he saved money by letting some knitters go. But quickly it turned into something else. Eddie and Louis began extorting the shopkeepers, likely their plan all along. I couldn't get clear details from Sam on how they did this, but I presume they threatened violence. No different than small time mafia. They were making money from sales of the sweaters, which as I understand it wasn't insignificant (but if done legally could have been a cover), and cash extortion of shopkeepers. Then they turned on Sam and demanded cash from him.

This was yesterday?

No, this had been going on since last July, but yesterday something else happened. Sam seemed exhausted. Still, I didn't offer him a drink.

I advised that he would have legal problems in front of him. I am always direct and honest with clients. This wasn't a small matter even if he could be shown to be the victim. Sell, or close right away? I scribbled on my pad.

I offered a change of venue, to the living room. A cigarette? No, he wanted to stay in the kitchen. Just as well. The phone rang but I ignored it. And so, yesterday?

Because something had to be done with the boy Sam hired Monte to work at the mill. After the war he had gotten into drugs, dealing, the street. His family didn't know what to do. "No one seemed to be able to do anything," he told me. So he did something, recognizing at the same time that he was exposing Monte to danger—danger for himself, Sam, and danger for Monte, for which he would never be forgiven.

Friday afternoon Eddie and Louis made new demands. In essence, they demanded control of the company. This is what frightened you?

Yes, he said. No, he corrected himself. It was the specter of Monte, who followed Eddie and Louis into Sam's office. Monte had affixed a strip of masking tape to his jacket. On it, he had written, in all capital letters, "DR. DEATH."

Sam Silk

I needed to know that none of this would get back to Harriett and Paul. Could he assure me? Naturally it might be difficult. Albert is Harriett's brother. Not forever, I promised him. Long enough to work things out.

Albert made a big deal about his damned coffeemaker. He sensed my nerves and tried to distract me. Albert recognized that he had a job to protect me and the company and by extension the family. He is a very fine attorney. For him to do this job I had to tell him as much as I could. Well, it will all come out in the end, won't it? My mother would say, in the dirty laundry.

The facts are the facts and I tried to lay them out without listening too carefully to myself. Albert needed the rough outline, the sequence of events that had led me to his kitchen on a Saturday morning at the start of June. I probably smoked three cigarettes sitting there. He lit them for me with a brass Zippo lighter. He is a polished character.

As I related the story of the past three years at Silk Industries, attempting to be honest with him and myself, I kept getting a picture of a broken man. This was disturbing. How had it come to this? I asked myself. Was this all my doing? Is it too late?

The longer I talked the more these questions bothered me. It turned out I wasn't getting anything off my chest. The pressure was building. The longer I spoke about Eddie and Louis and the terrible things they had done that I had been complicit in, willingly or not, as surely anyone could see, the more I wanted to talk about Monte. Did Albert see it, the danger I'd put him in? Monte, I tried to explain, has two sides, two sides of the same person, the artist and the operator. And the side of him that is the operator has two sides. One of these sides makes him a master mechanic, capable of freeing my mother from the bathroom or fixing a knitting machine that no one has used in eight years or, I imagine, saving lives on the battlefield. And the other is a killer. More than once I have sat in my office this last month and thought, Sam, he's going to kill you. That's why I ran from the office after lunch on Friday. The look on Monte's face as he entered my office behind Eddie and Louis was the look of a killer.

Did the war do this? When he was a student in her class did Harriett ever notice his eyes shift to the far distance, to some other place no one else could see? I was responsible for him now. I'd put him there. Immediately, he'd shown his value to Eddie and Louis. He could fix things. He could also convince a shopkeeper to do what he wanted. Sales in April were up. Louis had more cash in his hands than he'd ever seen. But what if he gets caught? Or what if Louis gets tired of Monte or gets his back up (it's obvious he will)? Christ, what will they do to Monte?

I tried to keep my composure. Albert, with his usual precision, wrote everything down. Naturally, he interrupted a few times to ask a question or make a legal suggestion. I imagined his neat handwriting on the pad, the careful lines piling up on top of each other. My story of destruction of the family legacy and his careful pen, the handwriting revealing nothing. The handwriting as cold as Monte's eyes.

He suggested we move to the living room with the great view over the square. But I wanted to stay in the kitchen. I couldn't handle the distance. Albert thought I needed a drink. I could tell. I refused to say anything. I was finished. I had nothing left to say. I closed my eyes.

Albert is as subtle as he is discrete. He asked about my mother. For ten or fifteen minutes he led me through the options. Round-the-clock care, a nursing home, move into our house. The third was no real possibility but needed to be acknowledged. Her assets could be distributed before her death to avoid tax liabilities. These are the kinds of things we discussed. Banal but necessary, meant to calm my nerves. Everything can be handled.

Everything can be handled. Albert used that exact phrase before proceeding with his counsel. The first thing I must do before examining the other courses of action is fire Eddie and Louis. Cut them loose. Albert will send the termination notices to their residences. He asked for their addresses, which I knew from memory:

Eddie Williams
615 Christian Street
Philadelphia, Pennsylvania
19147

Louis Turner
725 S. Smedley Street
Philadelphia, Pennsylvania
19146

Then he said I had an option. Close the mill, which would take some time, rectify accounts, and put the complex up for sale. Turn the page, in other words. In this case I would have to let all the employees go, including Monte. Or I could retain the core, legal business, and build from there, with Monte or not. Dammit: I refuse to believe there is no way to salvage what I care about most.

21.

Elsa Confirms a Hunch

Elsa Franklin Smith

My room is at the front of the house on the second floor. In the bay window over the porch I have a nice old desk. Charlene used this desk when she was a little girl and would write me letters I would receive the next day at my house halfway across town. One time, I received one of these letters the same day she sent it. I called her up I was so excited and she said, "Granny, send one back! See if it will come today, too." We had so many games, she and I.

The bay window allows me to look in three directions, up or down the block or straight across the street, and that's how I know what's going on. People will say, Miss Elsa, how can you see in the dark? There's no street lamp on your block. And I'll say, when it's dark and quiet in here, everything out there is bright and loud as day. You don't think it's true? You try it on your block. It's all the same everywhere. Only people are lazy or half asleep or they're watching the television. They got the television on day and night and they forget to look.

I don't know what these kids are up to, but both of them are out all night. I can tell you exactly when they come home, though. Jeanette gets in around one-thirty or two on the nights she's out, which isn't every night, mind you, and Monte about three. Jeanette races up the stairs with a backpack on her shoulder. I can hear her shoes clacking the marble steps. She takes them off inside, but still she runs right upstairs and I smile to myself about the energy of that girl. Monte slides in almost silent. He thinks no one on West Columbia sees because the car that drops him off pulls up on Lebanon Avenue. I can see Lebanon directly out the bathroom window. He crawls up the stairs and shuts his door with a whisper and a click.

The car that drops him off is a long red Cadillac with a leather top. Once, during the day, it pulled up on Columbia Avenue, idled for a while in front of the house, and pulled away. Another time, at night, it came around our block, hesitated in front of the house, and pulled around to Lebanon. Then, no more than four or five minutes later, Monte slid inside. That time I got a look at the driver of the Cadillac because he got out, came around to the passenger side door, and opened it for Monte. The man driving the car wore a long, black leather jacket.

I have suspected it a long time. Monte likes men but I'm not sure loves himself.

Monte Johnson

Who is this blood in the mirror? Tender-lipped faggot? Who made you that way? Daddy make you that way? Mama? Ninth grade health education? Tenth grade dance? Charlene? Her Jew-boy? Napalm, then? Saigon, then? Everyone fucks everything. Fucks a hole in the dirt, fucks a goat, fucks an ox, fucks a lost quiet thing, could be your sister. Medic has special powers, special touch, he check you, he cure you, he take small payment. This no homefront, this war. Try it yourself. You see. Now quit the lying, Medic. Medic? No, Monte I. Johnson, West Columbia Avenue, Overbrook, second floor middle bedroom, thimble window, no breeze. Just this lousy mirror, Kresge $1.99. Who is this blood in the mirror, three-thirty in the morning? Why he out so late? Listen? Is that the quiet? All the quiet but the reeds in the wind, the frogs, the chickens, all the quiet but Tuan's whisper, shh, Mrs. Tuan stirring. No this 13th and Locust, blood. Look down, not Rue Tu Do, no geisha, "Where you going? Come back right now!" I'm going, see? I got feet, bony ass feet and they sure as hell know where they're going. South. Pool Hall, Washington

Avenue, but you think I'm telling you? I ain't telling you. Pool hall they all in white undershirts, peanut skin, let me look, no touch, let me win, buy me beer, rice wine, five minute massage. Tuan? Tuan? Tuan? No one can find me there. But shit, what's that? The Cadillac jammed up on the curb. I'll walk, no thanks. Medic Johnson specialty trained to walk forever, Washington to Lebanon, capice? Honey, I don't want your leather jacket. I don't need it! "Get in the car, baby." It wasn't like that, was it? You got me home, but that's it. I ain't your tender-lipped faggot. I ain't! Don't need a sugar daddy, don't want protection, don't need.

22.

Little Monster Birds

Louis Turner

Monday comes, June 7, and Eddie picks me up in his Dodge Rambler. You can hear that junker from 21st and Snyder. We got plans! I get the radio off of 1060. The whole United States military coming to protect us from longhairs on July Fourth. Like George Washington and those other white crackers didn't have long hair. "Why you listen to that, Eddie?"

"I like to be informed," he says, like a proper Manager of Operations.

"I'm the only news you need."

"Can't turn you off." Mr. Eddie is like this.

"Man, don't you ever try."

"The Boss's mother's place is a goldmine. So imagine what you can't see."

"Don't be a fool," he says.

"OK, then me and Krishna split it. Up to you. I plan to retire, lay back."

"Uh-huh," he says.

"I already started casing the joint."

"The boss see you there?" All of a sudden he was interested.

"No, the boss didn't see me there. Anyhow, he can't fire me."

"For shaking down his mama."

"Krishna, not me. He got the touch." Eddie's on the Schuylkill now and I close my eyes. Roll down the window when we stop in traffic. The sun hitting my face. "Don't move, Eddie, don't move."

Boss is silent this morning. Pulls the Mercedes out of the garage, gets out, goes around to the passenger seat, and that's it. No cup of coffee. "No deliveries today, got it?" he says all hush.

Eddie nods, yes boss.

Boss goes on about inventory and "getting a handle on the product line."

I start thinking I'll slip out and head over to the Lebanon Arms. Lots of ways of making money. Can I take Krishna? No, that's a mistake. I don't want him to know anything until the time. When the time comes. I got to wait until the time comes.

Harry Silk

Did I tell you the one about the *shvartze*, a little guy with a face like a black turnip like they have in the old country? You're already laughing, but it ain't a joke, kid. I'm coming back from a trip to the Penn Fruit on Bryn Mawr Avenue with a box of Ritz crackers and a can of pink salmon and what's on my mind? The Phillies are 34-14 and already they're six-and-a-half games ahead. Is this the planet earth? I'm going to eat my cat's snack late tonight and watch the Phillies beat that rubber-arm Tommy John.

Crossing Wynnefield Avenue, I think, Harry, be careful. This isn't science fiction. It's the Phillies. They'll find a way to blow it. I come up to our drive and turn in. They have a little sidewalk that leads up to the front door and right beside that sidewalk, a hedge for the birds to play in. Little monsters make a racket. (I told the super this one time just to see what he would do and he smiled that stupid smile of his and I suggested a top brand of rat poison and he said he'd look into it. "You don't have to look into it, I'm telling you right now," I say, and he gets out his little notebook and pretends to write, the *meshuganah*.) And this is when I notice that it isn't the little monster birds but the *shvartze* with the turnip head. What's he hiding in those bushes for?

What do you think I'm going to say next? I'm a veteran—I got medals upstairs to prove it. He's up to no good, that much should be clear to you already. I could call the super, and what's he going to do? "Buddy, we got benches on the lawn. I'll give you the crossword and a pen," I say. And what does he say? "I already finished the crossword, you old coot." I'm just about starting to like this turnip head.

Does he have a pistol in his hand? He's pointing something at me through the pocket of his jacket as if I'm supposed to be impressed. If I worried about every nut job with a pistol in his pocket who walked into Silk Hardware I'd have been out of business in 1956.

"Why you talking so much?" he says.

And I say, "Did you hear the one about the…" (I had a good one to tell him about a nun, a rabbi, and an Indian chief) and now he's making it clear what's in his hand. What's he going to do, shoot me? What would I care? So I don't get to eat the Ritz crackers and pink salmon at least I won't have to suffer the Phillies.

Then, thanks to God almighty, I notice his sweater, light blue with navy stripes, makes him look fatter than he already is. "You're wearing a sweater made by the legendary Silk Industries," I say.

"What?" he says and so I repeat myself. "Tricky old Jew!" he says, as if I turned right there into the ghost of my brother Abe. He tries to squeeze through the bushes and the little monsters squeak and fly away. Now I'm in the elevator. "Next stop eight," I say. It doesn't matter to me I'm all alone.

Louis Turner

I'm not gonna shoot you, you old mule. Just go inside, forget it. White people always eating right out of your pockets. Like it's any of his business what I'm doing there. But then he says something about my sweater. How does he know where it was made? Must be some kind of omen, a sign. Shit, I don't miss signs.

Then I get home and an hour later Eddie calls. "You seen?" he says.

"Seen what?"

"The letter, return receipt."

"What letter?" I don't know what the hell he's talking about.

"Check your mail, fool," he says.

"Hold on." I put the receiver on the table and go out to the front radiator. That's where the guy who lives on the second floor puts everyone's mail. Damn, if there isn't a return receipt envelope from a lawyer, some Jew, "Birnbaum and Associates."

"You read it?"

"I only got two hands and two feet."

"The boss's wife's brother," he says real fast. He's excited.

"Who?"

"Birnbaum."

"This says I been fired."

"Cut loose, Louis, you and me."

"Shoulda popped that old coot."

"Keep your cool. There's money in the envelope." Damn that Eddie surrenders faster than a scared shopkeeper.

"You think he knows what he's asking for?"

"You knew it couldn't last. Probably got word the cops were onto him. So he's saving us, giving us cover. Be smart, Louis."

"You got Krishna's number at home?"

"Why?"

"Never mind, I know where he lives," I mutter.

"Boss took care of us for a long time." Damn, Uncle Eddie.

"Boss knew the game was up, Eddie. Use your head. We made the business. Otherwise he'd be closed up, gone."

"Wait it out. There's enough here—"

"Come here in the morning, just like normal."

"Why?"

"So we can shoot the shit, Eddie. I'll go to the Koreans and get some donuts. They got coffee, too."

23.

Sons of Sam

Monte Johnson

1. Sam Silk has paid my salary ($200 per week) since April 1.

2. April fools! I didn't start at Silk Industries until April 5.

3. Delivering sweaters to every last crazy ass bodega in Philadelphia I earned some additional cold, hard cash.

4. People like to live more than they like the money in their pocket (or cash register).

5. Sam has agreed to pay me $75 more per week to compensate for losing that business line.

6. Jewish people hate injustice as much as regular white people hate black people.

7. Jewish people like to live more than regular white people (they don't believe in the afterlife) and more (by a score of 51-49) than they like justice.

8. The P.L.O. gets crazy about this idiosyncrasy.

9. I am like a son to Sam (since June 8th). He goes crazy over my drawings of sweaters for the fall 1976 "Silk Line."

10. Louis Turner (lead in the water).

11. Krishna means black in Sanskrit. He is a giver of life, avenger of evil, a killer, and a joker.

12. I stay sober during the day. Sam does not.

13. (Still Lucky 13) I am more than a son to Sam?

Sam Silk

No, nothing is going to happen to me. Eddie and Louis aren't stupid. Monte's put away the Dr. Death routine. Now I pick him up in the morning and we talk about the business, how my grandfather hoped one day his two sons would take over and how good business was then, even, if you can believe it, better during the Great Depression than it is now. His grandparents' sold their grocery in 1965. They sold it for a profit. He stocked the shelves when he was eight or nine. Naturally, he helped Elsa make the displays, write up the advertising specials. When the grandfather took ill, he started going there after school every day. He'll tell me about Vietnam when he's ready, but for now he talks about the grocery store. Sometimes we don't say much, but the silence isn't harsh or heavy. We drive east, into the sun, and I reach over to pull down his visor.

I want to teach him things. But I know we have to go slow. You can't force it. Don't push him into a corner. Already he's teaching himself to design by adapting the old sweater line for the fall. If we can make it we'll have a new line. I'm still alive, dammit. This will be the first complete new line since 1970. I watch him draw, absorbed in it. For a minute I forget Eddie and Louis and the banks. Albert doesn't exist. Harriett doesn't exist. The mill. The drawing room. The knitting machines. Silk Industries. Monte and me. It's all a goddamned fantasy.

One bank is put off for now, but the other won't be for long. Albert wants me to close the business, liquidate everything. Get what I can. I have to figure out how to handle all the customers, the little stores that Eddie and Louis and then Monte had been extorting. Those people were scared for their lives. That's the only thing that kept them from coming after me. But what if they're no longer afraid?

Monte finished for the day. I offered to drive him home. No, he had somewhere to go. I don't know where he goes when he leaves here. I called my sons to see if they wanted to visit their grandmother. I could only get a hold of Paul (Alan must be avoiding me). Paul was willing to go. He always loved his grandmother. I told him I'd pick him up outside the Inquirer building at a quarter past six.

Betty Silk

The girl said someone was here. "Are they important?" You get to be my age and there's no sense in wasting your time. Most of them want your money. You can't be too careful these days. She said they were someone. "Important?" Very important. "Get me dressed, will you?" I had to look my best. "And hurry up."

Finally I came out to greet them. It was Abe and a colleague, I think our attorney. But he wasn't dressed very well. "You should have on a shirt and a tie!" I told that man. These days they go out in their pajamas. The lawyer got up. He said something about a box of chocolates. I called to the girl to get the nice crystal bowl out. Abe wanted to talk business. I could see he was thinking something over. What is it, dear? A new customer? An employee giving you a hard time? Come closer so I can see you.

The girl put the chocolates on the table. "Nana, have one," said the lawyer. My clever grandson, Paul. I grabbed two and put both of them in my mouth. I couldn't understand why Abe was arguing with the lawyer. It isn't like him. Abe, my angel, have a chocolate. He usually has such a sweet tooth. I don't know what they were arguing about. I closed my eyes. I opened them and there was the boy, Paul. "Did you take the streetcar all this way, dear? The 42? Turning awfully dark on that line. You have to watch your things."

He said, "Nana, don't talk that way." Then he said, to change the subject, I'm no dummy, that his brother Alan is having a party for the Fourth of July. "A party in the sky," he said, to watch the Bicentennial. "No bombs, Nana." I didn't know what he meant.

"Should I come?" I asked the boy.

"Oh, yes," he said, "no one should miss the Bicentennial."

Sam Silk

Harry was sitting in the kitchen listening to the radio and eating Ritz crackers. But not a crumb on the table. He has always been fastidious. Nephew, he calls me. He asked me to sit, have a cracker with some pink salmon. Right out of the can. I said we were down the hall, Paul and I. Join us for chocolates. The apartment was sweltering. Harry was too damn cheap to turn on the air conditioning.

He opened a can of salmon and put it on the plate with the crackers. He called it a cat's snack and chuckled. Christ, I had to sit down, eat the salmon on top of the chocolate still on my palette. I found a napkin and wiped my brow. Harry began a story about a man with a turnip head and a gun in his pocket. Turnip head was his exact phrase. I knew I would be there a while. Right there on Wynnefield Avenue? In the driveway? It took me a while to realize what he was saying had really happened. Harry said every single word of it was true.

Harry Silk

I had to get it through my nephew's head I wasn't going over there right then. For one the girl turns the air conditioning way up. The place is like an icebox in the summer and a coal furnace in winter, all the way to May Day. For two, I don't want to talk about this stuff around the kid, even if he is a newspaper reporter (let him stay innocent) or his grandmother, who never believed anything bad anyone told her because she didn't have to, thanks to my brother Abe, may he rest in peace.

I put out the cat's snack for him and as that usually works I started telling the story. I didn't need to tell him what happened blow-by-blow. So what? Nothing came of it. But I say, just to provoke him, "I've seen the face of evil and it has a turnip head." Sam is probably like his mother, glides along. But he fought the Nazis, don't forget.

"Were Nazis evil?"

"Well, Hitler—"

"Not Hitler, Himmler, Goebbels, Göring, everyday Nazis. Frau and

Fraulein Nazi. I dream of them, nephew, in their pigtails and braids."

"They were duped just the same. Some were victims, too."

"Show me which ones."

You probably don't agree, either. I see whose side you're on. You disagree about the turnip head, too. Fine. You're right, I had to say something to get me out of going into that icebox. He might not be evil, but he is a joker and jokers wear disguises, the good ones and the no-good ones. This one, I told my nephew, wears a Silk sweater.

Paul Silk

My father wanted to have a look at something so we went down the drive of the Lebanon Arms all the way to the street. What was it? He said it was nothing, nothing. "Everything is nothing," I said, "but nothing is nothing." The air was fragrant. Was it honeysuckle? Jasmine? Lilac? "So I don't believe you." He had his hands in his pockets, the light blazer flared out like it had wings, a pigeon's wings. The soles of his loafers ground against the asphalt. "I don't believe you."

He put his hand on my arm and turned us back toward to the street. We made a left to Lebanon Avenue. The car was in the apartment house lot. "The old neighborhood."

"Do you come here?" I asked. "You miss it."

"Only to visit my mother."

"But you miss it."

Hands still in his pockets, caught up in thoughts, he didn't answer. Then he handed me a drawing Monte had done. A new line. It was rough, in my assessment. I handed it back.

"You couldn't pay the bank?"

"No, I could. I paid."

"You paid with dirty money."

"Paid."

"You were looking at something back there?" I'd become a reporter again.

"The birds in the lilac bush," he lied.

"I don't believe you."

"For Christ's sake, nothing."

Then he stopped walking and said Harry had confronted a man in a Silk sweater with a gun. The man must have been his now ex-employee Louis and why was he there? To rob Nana's apartment? To take her hostage? Was he capable? "I tried to do the right thing for people—" I told him to alert the doorman. At least tell the doorman! Harry already had. Security was on alert. "I let it happen."

"You let what happen?"

"I let it happen. Things happened."

"Things happened? You mind elaborating?"

"I can't get into it."

"Can't or won't?"

"Let's go back to the car."

"You don't want to walk a little—the old neighborhood. Go over to the old house?"

"No, Paul. I washed my hands of it."

But his hands were stained, weren't they. We got back in the car and drove across the city line. Then he opened his window. He stuck his hand out and I could hear him tapping on the door. Whatever beat it was I couldn't make it out.

Sam Silk

It wasn't like talking to Albert, scribbling notes, angling in for a legal strategy. This was my son. I didn't want his forgiveness. No, to put it simply: He needed to know that his father had been complicit in his own demise. But I couldn't say it: A man heads in one direction and ends up in the opposite place. I went along with Eddie and Louis. They were terrorizing people, shaking them down. I let them shake me down! They shook me down but it didn't matter because the mill survived. They even drove me home at the end of the day to prove it. They needed the cash, anyway. Someone ought to put the blacks in charge, reverse the whole goddamned history. That's the only chance.

He kept pressing me. That's his job. Did I want to see the old house? Because he knew if we started walking the words would come

178

out. These streets will do that. But I knew what he was up to. And the birds in that bush making the clatter. I know what Louis was after. I'd let him in. I'm complicit in the whole damn thing. He really wanted to walk to the house. I could have said yes. I could have told him everything.

I'm not ready. I took the place over in 1961. Fifteen years later it's gone? Albert says go over there and close the place down. But what about the Federation of Teachers? Conrail? You can't let real money go. And what about Monte? I owe him more than Paul, Albert or anyone. In my jacket pocket was a folded-up piece of drawing paper. I'd forgotten I'd brought it to show my mother. Any little thing to excite her, to liven the day, but Harry had distracted me. This was one of Monte's drawings for the Fall Silk Line. I thought she would like the bold color. He learned quickly. We stopped in the middle of Lebanon Avenue. Paul held the drawing up into the light. He knew something about art. His section at the *Post* covered fashion design. Why not sell the designs? Why not? Silk Industries has always evolved. I tried to tell him I just need a little more time.

24.

Monte's Prayer

Monte Johnson

Inside the dark confessional of Saigon Notre Dame Cathedral.

Forgive me, Father.
Vietnamese please.
This is a French church.
Then why don't you speak in French?
I'm going to whisper, Father. Can you hear?
Try me in Latin.
Cet homme Sam Silk, *c'est un bon homme, grand homme, Père.*
M'écoutez? Sauvez-le, s'il vous plaît.
Sauvez-le de qui?
Sauvez-le.
Je vous bénis, mon fils.

25.

The Bicentennial Arrives

Charles Johnson

World Series Champs—1976 Phillies! It's really happening, right?
This must be it, the Bicentennial year. The man upstairs has got it
figured out. Seven games up on June 15. Who can beat 'em? Not the
Mets (that's for damn sure, putting moon man Mickey Lolitch on
the mound and praying), not the Pirates, not even the Los Angeles
Dodgers. Look at that swagger, big bats! The Bull!

Yeah, a lot of bull. This team's been playing how many years? Almost 100, you think they would have won one World Series, maybe
a fluke or something, an accident, maybe a forfeit. Nah. Not once.
And this team has fans? I mean, on what block? Nowhere on my
route. So don't believe it.

I tell you what, the centerfielder and the second baseman are
something to watch. But Cash's not exactly Jackie Robinson. He's
all right (look at that kid the Yankees got at second—keep your eye
on him). And I like the shortstop. He plays ball. I've been watching
him. Little guy knocks in a lot of runs. I see why they like the third
baseman. Boom, boom, boom, I see it.

Company sends out these little notes. They hand them out in the
cafeteria. Look at our team! And they're organizing Tasty Baking
Night at the Phillies. Not like the tickets are free, you still got to
buy them. The t-shirts are free, that's all. The t-shirts that advertise
their company. And with that emblem, little guy William Penn and

sweet old Betsy Ross playing ball. No thanks, I'll watch on TV. My back's aching too much to sit in those hard seats.

Now, they got something else going in the letter to us employees, especially to the delivery guys: Be advised, personnel will be required for certain functions during the citywide celebration of the Bicentennial, of which Tasty Kake is a proud sponsor. On July 4, 1976, two hundred years since the founding of our great nation, Tasty Baking will be there with our world famous Krimpets for everyone in the crowd to enjoy, our gift to America. Some bullshit like that, which means I don't get my day to take it easy. I served in both fronts because I love my country, but I can't get that. I got to be hauling boxes of Krimpets from the truck. I bet we don't even get to hand them out. I know that for a fact. That's not who does it. And who's gonna be there, anyway? I hear the news: Rizzo exposed himself this time. Terrorist plot my ass. They got 211,000 people to sign that recall petition. You think it will matter one damn second? That cat's not going anywhere. The whole city, like the baseball team, is cursed.

When Charlene was taken from us I told myself, no sense getting bitter now. Don't do it, Charles. You stay cool.

Paul Silk

More than 200,000 people want to recall the Mayor. I met some of them reporting "The Real Bicentennial Spirit." They weren't Mickey Mouse, Al Capone, or Snow White and the Seven Dwarfs, as Rizzo claimed so callously, proving all the while his capacity for lying on any subject, usually with impunity. "Lies are the weapon of the autocrat," I wrote in the story, which made the front page on Sunday. Most of "the signers," as I called them, had never participated in democracy before.

Mr. Rizzo thought fear of "domestic violence" would put the recall to rest. It backfired. The military rejected his request for troops. There never had been evidence of a plot against the Bicentennial. "The blood is on their hands," he said in response twelve days before July 4. Who would come? Sixty bands had cancelled. Hotels all of a sudden had openings. Maybe none of that mattered, if 200,000 had signed. That was the number that mattered. The city was utterly on the precipice, on more than one, on several, and some seemed dangerous and others maudlin and others wondrous.

The run of *Freedom* began on Saturday night. I sat in the back of the sold-out theater. Today, a week later, July 3, they've played five shows. A critic called it "new-age nonsense." Susan said was that was a sign of success, "if the old generation can't understand it."

This morning I took my mother's powder blue Buick (with the white top and white seats) to Simone's house on Pelham Street in Mount Airy to water the plants while she's away and to Nana Betty's in Wynnefield to make arrangements to get her to Alan's office to watch the Fourth of July parade. Already in the car, I went across the River to East Falls and across to Kensington as if heading to an autopsy. My father wasn't at home. Was he here, on a Saturday? Had he shut the mill; was Silk Industries closed? Or had he filed bankruptcy papers, if only to delay the inevitable? Had he come clean? I couldn't be sure of anything. In Kensington the air was eerie, hot, silent, as if the neighborhood baker had dropped dead and his oven kept cooking.

My father's car was in its spot as I had thought for some reason it might be. The office door was unlocked and the lights were on, but I didn't see anyone. I waited a while there in the same room where as kids Alan and I would file accounts, eat pastrami sandwiches from the deli, play around with the samples. The silence here was different because it mingled with my own thoughts and memories. I had a vague notion to write it all down, but the heat made even the thought of that drip away.

After a while I wandered out of the office and down the dusty wooden hallway toward the old, unused looms, in the original build-ing. Is he out to lunch? At the corner taproom? But there were foot-steps. Where? Right above? Everything in the old mill groaned, the city itself in death throes, or perhaps awakening. Up the stairs in the giant open loft. In the far corner of the empty space three drawing tables, a lamp dangling from the ceiling. What was this room before? The warehouse? Yes, now I recall boxes of sweaters, socks, scarves

185

going back to the 1930s. What had happened to all those boxes? It was a museum.

In the far corner: my father, standing, with a serious and concentrated expression, with his hand on Monte's shoulder. Monte sitting, statuesque, on a metal stool. Maestro and protégé. Then my father seemed to dance around. This wasn't the beleaguered Sam. He was doing what? Directing Monte. No, he was pacing and Monte was working. Monte only appeared statuesque, still, but his hand was washing across the paper.

As I got closer I saw there were several drawing tables and various sheets of paper, transparencies, pens, and watercolor. I apologized for interrupting. My father started showing me Monte's work, one design after the other, improving over the page he had shown me on Lebanon Avenue.

Monte, did he say anything? This was the first time I'd seen him since "the incident." He looked a bit more like his old self, fuller in the face, like Charlene, and with same angular cheekbones drawing all the energy down through the lips. Then finally he did speak. I had to close my eyes. "Paul," he said, "my brother straight out of stage left." I didn't have any idea what he meant.

Monte Johnson

There are no accidents.

Paul my brother came to me because he had to and I needed him to and most of all Sam needed him then. People only do things because they need to.

With my eyes I told Paul to meet me downstairs, in the office of the Operations Manager. He is dense, thick as the Mekong jungle, and so I had to say it out loud: Paul, I want to show you something downstairs. Sam, I'll be right back.

I let him go first down the stairs. He grew up here. The mill was his.

You wondering, Paul, why we're working on a Saturday. Holiday weekend. Bicentennial?

No, no. No need to answer.

You see this tape? And this second roll, just in case? It's not for boxes. It's to tie your daddy to the chair and threaten his life so that he will hand over every cent to my fools.

My fools: the dog Eddie and his tail Louis.

He asked: What?

Yes, I was supposed to lead Sam into a trap and then out of stage left you appeared. Impeccable timing, as always.

Rizzo's got the cops all distracted. No red car for miles.

Time to celebrate freedom, Paul. Listen to Monte: he's changed his mind. In the middle of battle you decide on the fly. Capice? Take your daddy out of here now.

You're saving him.

Yes, I'm saving him.

You, Monte?

What about me?

Save yourself, he said.

This isn't *Avengers*. I know how to get to the El. 13th Street is exactly sixteen minutes. All I got to do is worry about some white hoods, Snow White and the Seven Dwarfs? What can they do to me?

He said he was grateful. He looked at me with those decent eyes.

Paul Silk

"You're saving us," I said, "all of us."

"Then, go," he said, hard Monte again. "Then, go."

"No, we all stay," I declared.

"You don't fuck around."

"Then we all leave together."

"Then they set the place on fire," Monte looked at the floor.

"Then we call over to the station house."

"Then those freaks talk."

My father came down. I explained so Monte wouldn't have to admit what might have happened. Hands in pockets again. I looked to him, he looked to Monte, as if Dürer was standing there carving us.

"We're staying," said Monte. He went out into the courtyard.

We followed, like sweaty-palmed henchmen. My father was to pull his car out of courtyard and bring it around to Dauphin and find a place to park on the other side of the street. And stay there in the car. They won't realize the Mercedes isn't in the courtyard as they come up Emerald. "I know where they're coming from," Monte said.

I had to go the other way down Dauphin and steal the largest American flag I could find. "They'll never miss it, unless a blood takes it, then they'll miss the flag and the queen's diamonds. My brother: the widest-ass flag you can find. Pretend you really love your country." I was already halfway into the intersection. On the right side of the street, at number 2024, there it was, large enough to fly outside City Hall, and on a flagpole slotted just to the left of the door. "I'll bring it back," I said, to whoever wanted to hear.

Monte Johnson

My brother. Get another one, I'm going to teach you a drill. Here's your chance to serve. I sent him the other way. The kid will do anything for you.

It wasn't three minutes he was back. By my calculation we had no more than fifteen minutes and I prayed he could follow directions. Listen up, soldier. The Rambler's coming this way, over from 5th, down Diamond, up Front, and across right here on Susquehanna, which turns into Emerald. Eddie doesn't drive slow. Not with Louis bouncing like he's bucking Sally. You know? And so here we'll be, practicing our Bicentennial drill, like two old generals, stepping and waving our flags in salute. Right here and don't pay attention to anything else but the red, white, and blue that runs in your veins. Anybody comes out of the joint over there will think they better throw beer bottles at us, but they won't because they will see that we are serious. The flag is the flag and we are brothers. You, Paul, are Jeremiah and I'm Moses of the Israelites and when they see us parading, waving the flag real hard like it's a stiff wind and clicking our heels, understand, old Eddie's going to run right into that telephone pole. Bam-o. Smack into the pole, we disappear, and the officers of the law are here forty-five seconds after we jump into the Mercedes and roll away. And don't forget to prop the flag on the corner. You can't just toss it on the ground.

My brother. I never got to see you put that ring on my sister's finger. Don't look at me like that. This is a crazy ass plan and crazy ass plans are our only chance, you hear? Don't go weeping. Soldiers don't weep over nothing. You're a soldier now, Paul. You pull this off and I'll forgive you, that's how real brothers are.

Paul Silk

"They still could rat out Sam," he said, scratching his head. The afro seemed to grow in volume with the heat. "But they won't likely. And now they've made themselves known in the neighborhood. No, they got a ticket to pay and the front end to fix, at least this buys some time."

Eddie swerved the other way and almost killed a dog. Running down Emerald we heard the car's breaks and the screech that followed and the sound of glass. I think he hit the traffic light, which must have fallen right into the doorway of the taproom.

I ran over to 2024 Dauphin and replaced the flag and jumped into the car as my father rolled by. Monte was in the front seat. I stretched out on the leather seat and breathed in the brine of it. Leather has a strange way of smelling like sardines, especially in the summer when everything is hot and at the same time relieved of burden.

Charles Johnson

You know when you know, and I knew. July Fourth I got to work, and nothing I can do about it. Granny says call in sick. Call in sick? Who's she talking to?

I felt it in the truck on the way over. Five-thirty. The radio was on. I turned it up. No Rizzo, no Bicentennial, no Phillies, I don't care if they are thirty games over .500. No, just sweet Teddy. Every time I felt a tinge I turned it up more. Smooth it out. Empty streets. A cool breeze.

What we got. Hundreds of boxes of Butterscotch Krimpets. All of them going down to Independence Hall. Enough to feed every last white patriotic American. I should be standing there waving the flag and they should be serving me.

But it doesn't work that way. The fifth box off the forklift and into the truck. No, no! The sixth, seventh, and I was on the ground. Do me a favor, call my house. I need my kid to get me out of here. I can't move!

Elsa Franklin Smith

I told him. "Call in sick, they don't need you on the Fourth of July. They've been doing just fine for two hundred years." But Charles is hardheaded. That's how he puts up with Anita. They couldn't be married if he wasn't that way.

I watched him lumber out to the truck, moving real slow. "At least have an aspirin!" From the porch I told him to stop and I'd bring him a glass of water and the aspirin. I gave him two and he swallowed them.

Then it seemed like a minute later the phone was ringing. It was seven-thirty. I had bacon on before it got too hot out.

I didn't recognize the voice. A gruff voice. "Charles is down, can't move. It's his back. He wants his kid," the man said.

"What kid?"

"His kid."

"Monte, you mean?"

"Guess so. Tell the kid to go right to Hunting Park. Put his dad on the couch and tell him not to move."

This Bicentennial's bringing all kinds of trouble. Paul said Sam could pick me up and bring me to the party on the top of Alan's building. I said I could get there myself on the streetcar. Now, who's going to take care of Charles? His wife?

I went right upstairs and opened Monte's room. The child was sound asleep. I shook and shook him. "Get up! Your daddy's back went out on him. He needs you to go pick him up. He can't even walk!" I sat up and down on the bed to make it rock, like the ocean. Finally, his eyes opened. "He needs you!" Somehow that worked and he jumped out of bed. Monte has a body like a slack wire, but hook it up somehow it's live. "Go!"

I grabbed a couple slices of crisp bacon and handed him the keys to the car. "You'll have to lay him out on the back seat. And drive slow. Any bump could twist him up good!"

Paul Silk

I hadn't anyone to worry about but me. This was a false notion, a lie, and anyway I also felt exactly the opposite way, that I was responsible for everyone, for Monte, for my father, for Granny, Jeanette, for Charles.

Independence Day I got to Alan's building early and for a while was alone on the lookout terrace. Only a few tourists had paid to come up. The sun was high already and the sound of marching bands came and went as if the parade was going in and out of a tunnel.

Here we were on the precipice. The city on a precipice. People had come to celebrate. Thousands? Tens of thousands? Hundreds of thousands? Who could say? In the end they didn't abandon the city, not completely. They couldn't, I suppose, like some blind force. Yet they'd come hesitantly, as if walking toward a dream. I thought of the people down on the street and the signatures on the recall petition. Who was dreaming of the city past and who the city future?

A French horn blared aberrantly, interrupting. It threw me back into the moment. My father, Sam Silk, surely on the precipice. Had Eddie and Louis been arrested? Louis has a big mouth, I gather. I wanted to call Albert myself and ask the questions that needed to be asked. Will Albert be here today? Alan wasn't sure. "He shows up when he shows up."

I told him that Dad was to pick up Nana Betty and bring her here, probably around three. He gave me the phone number to the terrace in case there was a problem. Not everything should be left to chance. Could she even make it? At least there is air conditioning inside the terrace and plenty of food supplied by Alan's company.

The President was to speak from a podium down below. Someone said the parade was going to be five hours or longer. Rizzo had scared away more than half the bands. Someone else said, maybe we should thank Rizzo, after all.

Sometimes this city devours itself.

I went inside for a while to get out of the heat. I sat in a black leather chair of high design and drifted to sleep.

When I woke up I got a plate of food and went back to the terrace to watch the parade. I had a strange notion that this was the moment. I felt a gaze and I felt a sense of culmination. Not the end exactly, but a moment of gathering. With whatever's left we'll go forward. Somehow I'd missed the arrival of Jeanette and Granny. Jeanette had brought Granny on the streetcar and the old woman was leaning over the railing. She too must have felt something. I imagined it was exhilaration.

Alan came over and said Dad had called. "Traffic was so bad he got out of the car, walked to a pay phone, and dialed up here." They were stuck.

Jeanette was wearing Charlene's ring. Jeanette said that Charles had thrown out his back and that Monte had stayed with him. "He didn't even argue or say anything weird," she said. And then she leaned in and, speaking directly into my ear so that Granny couldn't hear, invited me to come watch her belly dancing performance later that night.

"Not tonight," I said, "I'll be too exhausted. But before summer is out." Jeanette said she couldn't wait.

It was that moment, when Jeanette's fingers slid off my shoulder and she went over to Granny, that I saw a small figure, in red, glimmering in the sun, her honey-colored hair puffing and collapsing like a bellows. The sun poured into the honey as the figure moved to its own internal rhythm. Susan said she wanted dance to break through the barriers, of space and expectation. Dance is movement and movement can also be still just like silence is its own kind of noise. Though the grand public space in front of Independence Hall was crowded, she seemed never to notice another creature.

Susan looked like a bird aware only of itself, the light, the earth and trees. My gaze, too, poured down on her, a physical sensation so powerful that I felt for the longest time watching her that we were connected, and that we could fly together.

Susan Painter

Once or twice I closed my eyes and felt the heat on my face and the people breathing in and out a kind of crazy, mixed-up love. And so I kept going. That was the plan, dance until I can't, until I've exhausted my body but not my body's freedom to move, to express itself.

Some time went by (I wouldn't dare guess how long). I could hear the band music faintly, and the sound of a vuvuzela, which someone kept blowing at odd increments of time. The vuvuzela was the only thing, like a clown laughing, that could break my reverie. But I didn't let it.

And then, dancing through the crowd in Independence Square, I had the strangest sensation, as if a person's gaze could have physical power. Of course it could, that's the energy of the universe speaking to me through Paul, his energy joining mine and I could feel his eyes on me. Not just his eyes, his gaze, the current of his existence. This might have frightened me who is so afraid of being trapped, but instead it poured over me like a steady, constant flow, a never-ending electric stream, and even now as I sit on the curb at 4th and Walnut, away from the mass of the crowd, I can still feel it, only now it seems to be reversing direction, pulling me (gently) to him, wherever he may be.

Charles Johnson

Someday somebody's gonna ask, why'd they make those cars so damn long? Like aircraft carriers of the streets? I'll tell you. So the front seats recline real long and low so some old cat who's thrown his back out can recline almost like he's lying on the couch.

Man I don't know how they did it but my son and Ed Laborski got me in there. Ed used to be a wrestler. Said he was leaving the rest of the boxes for me when I came back. Monte got Jeanette. He had to wake the girl while I lay there prone with the door of the

Continental open. Somebody was already setting off firecrackers. They got me and put me on the couch. All morning the kid's right there. Granny makes some toast, he brings it in, he sits in the armchair and all of a sudden he's talking about sitting on the balcony of a place in Saigon and the shutters are creaking. That's what Monte said he remembers, the shutters. What kind of a building: a house, he said, a geisha house. The kid was trying to tell me something. Shit, speak your mind! Shit. It kills if I think. When this is over, that's it. I'm done with the truck. I'm done sitting.

Sometime I got him to switch on the TV. No, I got it wrong. He switched it on, Phillies and Pirates, game one of a doubleheader. All day Monte was like this, like he knew exactly what I needed. He let his mother sleep and after a while his sister and Granny left out for the Bicentennial. It was the fifth inning. Carleton on the mound was faltering, hasn't been the same lately. Makes these facial expressions, like the devil's inside him and he's trying to chase him out. I was praying Pops would get to him, but Carleton is crafty, I admit. He even helped himself out with a single that knocked in the centerfielder. That's what you get when the best hitter is batting seventh. He singles, steals second, and the pitcher knocks him in. That made it eight to four and I shut my eyes. Monte finally found the heating pad. And when I woke up they were between games. Now if the Phillies won the first what do you think's about to happen? You think they'll win two for the Bicentennial? Not a chance, Monte said from the kitchen. My kid doesn't know anything about baseball, but he listens!

Might have been the fourth or fifth inning. Nobody wanted to score. Monte paces by. Hey Son, what do you think I should do? I can't sit in that truck no more. I dunno, he says. Get old? Not me. I ain't getting old. All you like is baseball. Yeah, so? Don't they have people take the tickets, show you your seat? They took us to a Pilots game, during training. You went to a ball game? Why you never tell me? They took our tickets, escorted us to the right place and wiped off the seats for us. Soldiers, that's why. Anyway, I can't bend over. Get to watch all night long, he answered. He walked away. That centerfielder's something to watch. Hey, Monte! He's back and forth to the kitchen, pacing around, started giving me a long and twisting speech about how he thought I should know about something but doesn't think it's a big deal and so on. Then it must be a big deal! What you talking about, kid? What you talking about? Didn't I know? Didn't I? I shut my eyes. Go ahead, speak kid! Everybody's got to live. Nothing I can do about it. Then he swallows himself. You're never gonna believe it but—But what, now? What? What's he want to tell me? Go on! Swallows everything, he's gonna make some shit up. This isn't it. But he goes on, pretending. Jeanette's got a gig at a Lebanese place belly dancing. She's the Nubian in the desert. She's belly dancing downtown. Don't worry, she's cool, no one touches her, just a show. Charlene's voice in my head saying look, look at your son. Look at him! I blocked her out so I could only hear Monte. Only Monte. That's all you got to say? She's gonna be a hygienist, too. The girl has dreams. Shit. I had to shut my eyes again. And I half-believed him.

Jeanette Johnson

Granny and I had been there almost an hour when Paul came out on the terrace with all the other people. I don't know where he'd been hiding. Alan asked if I liked his space age building. He showed me all the buttons and switches that turn everything off and on automatically and then he gave Granny and me a personal tour of the terrace and what we could see from up there and you could hear the marching bands go by. We were all waiting for the fireworks. Granny and I agreed that was the best part. "Oh, yes," she said, "we're staying all the way to the end." The bridge was going to be lit up, too. But they won't let us have sparklers up here.

I went inside and called Monte to see how Daddy was doing. "He's watching baseball is how he's doing. Something else to moan about." And then Paul appeared and he was holding Granny's hand. I linked my arm in his and we went to the edge overlooking the park. "You're coming to see me dance, right?" I whispered in his ear.

"Yes, yes, of course, sweet Jeanette, but not tonight. In a couple weeks."

"Our special Bicentennial show goes only until August. You better not miss it." Oh, poor Paul, I did want him to come, but now he looked like he was tormented. "You better not forget," I said. Granny had her eyes fixed on something out there. All the colors, Granny loves the colors.

"I hope you don't mind if I bring a guest," he whispered.

"You already asked me that, silly. Bring as many people as you want." Granny was clapping now. He cleared his throat.

"I'm bringing someone but she's busy for a couple more weeks," he practically swallowed all the words. I smiled. He smiled, a little afraid. I could have fallen down, if not for the railing. Then I got my legs. I took a breath. I wiggled and jiggled to calm down, get composed.

"Paul Silk, you're asking me if it's OK to bring a date?"

Paul's ears went red. I wanted to slap him across the face. I put my arms around his neck, kissed his cheek. Everybody's got to live. Charlene, you don't have to know. She doesn't know. Just as I started to get choked up it came to me we can make a deal, at least for tonight. "Since I got to go straight downtown to work after this is over you can take Granny home on the trolley. She better not go by herself." Paul, of course being Paul, squinted and he said nothing could make him happier in the world.

Paul Silk

A few minutes after we came out of the trolley tunnel we heard the fireworks, or firecrackers, from every direction. It felt like the trolley was under attack, but Granny never shielded her eyes or covered her ears. Kids seemed to be everywhere as the trolley lumbered up Lancaster Avenue and inside the car one was even dancing in the aisle.

I nudged Granny awake and we came down at 63rd and Lebanon. Had the street ever been this noisy? "It's a real hot night," said Granny, "real hot." She kept asking how I was going to get home. She offered Monte to drive me.

Charles had his legs up over the arm of the sofa. The TV was on.

Anita was out back smoking a cigarette. Monte was making something to eat. "Happy Independence Day," Monte said. His voice was his voice, as if a war had broken out between irony and earnestness. It could almost have been 1968.

"To you, the same," I said. It was too bad he couldn't have come down to watch the festivities.

"Old veteran needs me," Monte shrugged.

"I can't move from this spot," Charles said. His voice seemed to come from nowhere. What did he need? Granny said she was coming. "No, no! Medic Johnson's doing me all right. The Bicentennial's not gonna kill me."

Granny said she would finish in the kitchen so Monte could drive me home. "That's too much trouble," I said, "let me just use the phone." I dialed Nana's apartment. It rang for a while before my father picked up. They'd been caught in traffic all afternoon. After a while he gave up. They returned to the Lebanon Arms and watched the parade on TV. He said he'd pick me up.

About twenty minutes later he rang the bell and came inside. He kissed Granny hello, went out to the yard to greet Anita, and sat with Charles for a while, listening to Charles' story about his back going out and Monte and a guy named Laborski getting him into the car. "You got him in, but how did you possibly get him out?" my father asked. Charles laughed so hard he seized up in pain.

Monte, I noticed, had stayed in the kitchen. He had put some shrimp in a pan to sauté and some peanuts crumbled on top. My father went in to ask him something. "Your mouth watering?" Charles inquired, and so I couldn't hear what they were talking about in the kitchen.

When we walked down their stoop I said I didn't really feel like going home. If you drive—" His eyes lit up and he said, "I know where."

He directed me over to 52nd Street.

The radio was on. "Tens of thousands jammed Independence Mall...no violence, political or otherwise...none of what Mr. Rizzo had predicted, blood on the hands of the Federal government, which refused his request for National Guard...the parade of some 80,000 people went on for five hours in the summer heat...Speaking at

Independence Hall, President Ford…"

"He'll get away with it," my father said.

I wanted to ask, "Didn't you read my article?" But I said nothing. I turned off the radio instead.

We crossed Lancaster Avenue then Girard then Haverford. I slowed down as we neared Market Street and passed under the El. The conversation stayed like this, impersonal. "Are we sure we want to come down here?"

"Why not. It's the Fourth of July."

"OK, which place?" The street was lined with neon. Then I saw it: Mr. Silk's Third Base. "That one, naturally," I exclaimed.

"Can you believe I forgot about that place?"

"But you don't think?" "No, we're not going in there. Forget it." He said it was out of the question, the wrong crowd. "Keep going," he insisted.

"The Aqua Lounge, there we go." Flashing sign on the left. "They have valet."

"Yes. This is what I wanted," he explained. "But turn on Pine and come around and park behind. We don't need to pay."

"Sure?"

"We don't need the hassle," he said.

"It's supposed to be easier."

"Never is."

I followed his instructions and we found a spot in the neighborhood. Music was piped in. The band was on break. Almost quiet enough to talk. We ordered two Wild Turkeys. The walls were slick. Everything was slick.

"Better than the parade!" he said.

"Better than the parade."

He crossed his arms on the table. Then he opened them and I felt a wall crumble. First the paint then plaster then lathe. "I did all I could."

I nodded silently.

"Look at all the firms that went under years ago. Look at Stetson."

He couldn't face it. My father a coward. A coward who thinks he's brave. "You survived."

Red then white then blue light skimmed across his face. He was lost in the light.

"They're gone now," he said.

"Who?"

"Eddie and Louis—thugs."

"You made your decisions. Can't go back." Was my father listening? He was lost.

The glass of Wild Turkey sweated in his hand. And his forehead, too, was sweating. "This is a night for celebration."

Colored lights announced the next set. McCoy Tyner on piano. My father leaned back, closed his eyes. We ordered another round. "You don't ever forget this sound."

People kept piling into the Aqua Lounge. The air conditioning couldn't keep up. Faces seemed to rupture across the room. Over there, was that Monte, in the silk shirt? How could it be? He was home taking care of Charles. But isn't that him? Dad got up to look, slid through the crowd. Over toward the bar. His back to me. Was it Monte? Dad raised his arm. He hesitated, put it back. Now he extended it again, hand on Monte's shoulder. Was it Monte? Dad was lost in the crowd. The man turned sideways. I still couldn't see.

Sam Silk

Somehow I got the waitress's attention and ordered another round. Paul won't let it go. He blames me. But then just like that, what is it? Monte? Monte's here? I kept myself still. I didn't move my head or change my expression. I didn't turn to look. How could it be? He's at home with Charles. But just like that I got up, went over to see. Dammit, something strange has stirred me up. I slipped through the crowd toward the bar. It's him? No, a mistake, someone else. Someone who looks just like him. In the dark it's hard to see.

"Oh, no? Sorry," Paul said when I returned to the table. "I thought—but of course it wasn't possible."

Paul Silk

My father looked at me, defeated. He finished both our drinks.

"It doesn't matter," he said.

"What is it?"

He didn't respond. He turned to find the waitress again. He ordered another round.

"Somehow," I said, maybe to redeem my own family, "the night's turned sweet. Look around." The Aqua Lounge had a milky air.

"I've forgiven Monte everything," he said after a while.

I nodded.

"Your mother was right. He needs the utmost care."

"Of course. We all love Monte, don't we?"

Just one more round.

"He looks a little like Charlene, doesn't he?"

"Yes, down through the mouth."

"When she died did she have any idea what he'd been through?"

I didn't want to say it. "She thought he was dead, killed in Vietnam. Her last words—"

"I'm sorry. I'm sorry. He is very much alive. You know that. I know it, Paul. I want you to know. I know he's alive. Maybe he'll save us again."

In the heat and noise everything felt inscrutable. But through it I saw a man clawing at his knots. If only he could get himself undone. "I should drive," I said.

"Yes, you take the wheel, kid."

He gestured for me to pay. I left double the bill. It wasn't any cooler outside. Kids were still setting off firecrackers. A group of teenagers on the corner: what were they up to? We'd better go around the other way. "It's always been a little like this around here," Dad said. "You go one or two blocks in one direction—"

"Things change."

The car was gone. Empty space where it had been. Those kids? Who knows? You can't ask them. "I know where the police station is. It's been a long time, but I've been there."

The station was busy. We waited a few minutes and then the intake officer took our information. His badge said "Curran."

"Where from?"

"Delancey, 5100 block."

"You locked it?"

"Of course we locked it."

But had I?

"Plates?"

"KG7 434."

"Make?"

"Mercedes 220 Sedan."

"Color?"

"Cream," my father said.

"White?"

"More like rice pudding," I said.

"German cars are hard to steal. You sure it was locked?"

"It was locked, dammit." He looked beaten, as if nothing else would ever be the same.

"You have insurance? Better call them when you get home." Officer Curran kept his hat down low. "I'll send this over, but you probably won't see it again. Get yourself a new one."

"It's out there!"

"Like I said, I'd get yourself a new one."

"They don't make it anymore. A car's stolen, and you can't even try to find it."

"Don't put words in my mouth, mister." He was typing the report. He typed "Slik" then had to pull the sheet out, erase the misspelling with whiteout then type it again. He spit a wad of gum into a trashcan. Dad signed the form and waited to be handed a copy.

The officer gestured, "The pay phone's over there if you need to call a cab."

Appendix:
The Monte Decimal System

Monte Johnson

Class 000 Monte, Brain System of
   000 Circuitry, Basic
      001 Great Chain of Being, The
         001.1 Anatomy, False
      002 Biology, Evolutionary
         002.1 Anatomy, Probably Correct (Human)
   010 Knowledge
   011 A priori
      011.1 Kingdoms of Ghana
      011.2 Georgia plantation
         011.21 House knowledge
            011.211 Obedience
            011.212 Rewards
         011.22 Field knowledge
            011.221 Survival
            011.222 Musical transference
      011.3 Philadelphia, Ye Olde
         011.31 Streets, Wooden
            011.311 Wheelin' and dealin'
            011.312 Audacity
            011.313 Respect
         011.32 Streets, Brick

011.321 Lack of control
011.322 Learned inferiority
011.323 Victimhood
011.324 Silent hope
012 Knowledge, Conveyers of
012.1 Granny
012.11 No pity
012.12 Eternal love
012.13 Elegance
012.14 Self-respect
012.2 Sang, Tuan Van
012.21 To be and not to be
012.22 Peanut, Color and Smell of
012.23 Tenderness
012.24 Purity
012.25 Perversity
012.26 Uncontrollable sadness
012.3 Charlene
012.31 Admiration
012.32 Politics
012.33 Feminism
012.34 Abandonment
012.35 Fraternity
012.351 Keeper, Am I my Brother's
012.4 Daddy
012.41 Certainty
012.42 Uncertainty
012.43 Forget, How to
012.44 Honesty
012.45 Baseball
012.451 1951 New York Giants
012.452 Burden, Black Man's
012.5 Mommy
012.51 Forget, How not to
012.6 Silk, Mrs.

012.61 The Jewish mind
    012.611 Self-expression, Obligation of
    012.612 Fairness, Adoration of
012.62 Irony, Concept of
012.63 Tragedy, Meaning of
012.7 Jeanette
012.71 Fake it, How to
020 Sober
    021 Fantasies, Stupid
    022 Puns, Really bad
030 High
    031 Fantasies, Demented
    032 Fantasies, Dangerous
    033 Puns, Criminal
040 Dreams
    041 Nightmares
050 Medical
    051 Iodine, alcohol
    052 Splints, tourniquets, and bandages
    053 Tracheotomy blade
    054 Mercy
Class 100 (Reserved for Robot Monte)
Class 200 Monte, Religion of
    210 Religion
        211 Sacramental
            211.1 St. Peter Claver
            211.2 Our Mother of Sorrows
                211.21 Confession 1964-1968
            211.3 Sacraments, West Philly
                211.31 Blood
                211.32 Spit
            212.4 Sacraments, Saigon
                212.41 Blood
                212.41 Guts, gristle
                212.43 Spit

212.44 Cum
212 Rapturous
212.1 Mother Bethel
212.11 Granny—Easter 1959-1962
212.2 Good Book, The
212.21 Leviticus 15.1-16 (see 012.2 Tuan Van Sang)
212.22 Deuteronomy 21.1-8 (see 524 An Thanh)
212.23 Mark 7.24-30
212.24 Lamentations 5.22
212.25 Ephesians 5.12-13
212.26 Jude 8-16, 22-23
213 Buddha, The
213.1 Buddhism of the Brothel (Geisha) (see 522 Saigon)
213.11 Altar of Khak Hoi (Bitter)
213.12 Altar of Tu Do (Sour)
213.13 Altar of Vung Tau (Salty)
213.2 Buddhism of An Thanh (Bittersweet—see 012.2 Tuan Van Sang)
214 Judaism
214.1 Four Questions, The
Class 300 Monte, Bibliography of
310 White Pages, The (see 022 Really Bad Puns)
320 Overbrook High School
321 Overbrook HS Commencement Program 1969
322 *Overbrook Record*, p. 175
323 Debating Society Standings, mimeographed, April 3, 1968
324 "Protestors arrested at 52nd Street El Stop," *Philadelphia Bulletin*, August 7, 1968
330 U.S. Army
331 25th Infantry "Electric Strawberry"
332 *New York Times*, May 4, 1970 (photo)
333 Cambodia, list of undead soldiers
334 Vietnam, never declared MIA
Class 400 Monte, Languages of
410 Philadelphia

411 Modified Proud Black English (see 012.4 Daddy)

412 White English (see 012.5 Mommy)

413 Old Black Proud English (see 012.1 Granny)

414 English (see 012.3 Charlene)

415 College English (see 012.6 Mrs. Silk)

416 Homosexual English

417 Shakespeare

418 Black English

420 Vietnam

  421 Redneck English

  422 Creole

  423 Geisha house French

  424 Ambush English-Jive

    424.1 Dap

  425 Swamp Vietnamese

  426 Saigon Street French

  427 Broken English

  428 Graffiti

    428.1 uuuu

  429 Love and Despair, Language of (see 012.2 Sang, Tuan Van)

Class 500 Monte, Geography of

  510 Philadelphia

    511 Overbrook

    512 #10 Trolley

    513 Rittenhouse Square

      513.1 Dewey's 17th Street

    514 Washington Square

      514.1 Hasty Tasty

      514.2 Camac Baths

      514.3 Giovanni's Room

    515 Kensington

      515.1 Past

        515.11 "White Town"

        515.12 Silk Industries

      515.2 Future, Unforeseen

520 Army
 521 Hawaii
 522 Saigon
 523 Valley of the Reeds
 524 Vung Tau
 524 An Thanh
 523 Cambodia
 524 Ft. Lewis
530 (Denver)
540 Mother Russia (see 621 Russian)
Class 600 Monte, Literature of
610 Black
 611 Black, read by whites
  611.1 Baldwin, James
  611.2 Hughes, Langston
  611.3 Wright, Richard
  611.4 Ellison, Ralph
  611.5 Hansberry, Lorraine
  611.6 Testament, New
  611.7 Haley, Alex
  611.8 Hurston, Zora Neale
 612 Black, barely read by whites
  612.1 Johnson, James Weldon
  612.2 Quran, Al
  612.3 Ross, Fran
  612.4 Kelley, William
620 White
 621 Russian
  621.1 Pushkin
  621.2 Gogol
  622.3 Dostoyevsky
  622.4 Tolstoy
  622.5 Turgenev
  622.6 Nabokov
 622 Shakespeare